PRETTY, DARK & DIRTY

BY MARGOT SCOTT

M̲ | Independently Published

Edited by Kathleen Payne

ISBN: 9798608475641

PRETTY, DARK AND DIRTY

For all the Daddy's girls.

Visit margotscott.com to sign up for Margot's newsletter.

Follow Margot on Facebook at facebook.com/margotscottauthor

Prologue

When I was little, I suffered from frequent night terrors that led to a fear of sleeping with my back exposed. My father, awoken by my cries, would lift me from my crib and carry me in to sleep between my parents in their already too-cramped bed.

I don't recall the nightmares, but if I close my eyes, I can still feel the weight of my father's arm around me, and the solid presence of his chest against my back. The vague awareness of feeling safe, warm, and protected.

These days, I no longer need to close my eyes to remember how it felt to be loved.

I have only to slide my hand across the sheet to find another hand reaching out for me, or whisper, *Daddy*, in the dark to feel his arms enfolding me.

I came to the city in search of answers. What I found was a love I couldn't have known, had the truth been made plain to me from the start.

And had I known the price Mason and I would pay in my pursuit of the truth, I'm not sure I would've climbed on that bus—

But I did, and there's no going back now, for either of us.

Chapter One

I'll never forget the first time I visited the Metropolitan Museum of Art. I was four years old, holding my mother's hand in front of an immense portrait of George Washington. My toes pinched in my bunny-rabbit sneakers after hours of wandering through galleries, and I couldn't stop squirming in my itchy denim overalls.

Exasperated, my mother turned to my father and said, "Mason, just take her."

He hoisted me up and carried me off to the Egyptian wing, past the reflecting pool and into the Temple of Dendur.

"Look, Jetty," he'd said, using his nickname for me. My gaze followed his finger to the remains of a small statue encased in glass. "That's the priestess Tagerem, God's Wife to the Egyptian sun god Ra."

"What's a Ra?" I asked.

"One of the most powerful gods in all of Egypt. He rides a chariot across the sky during the day, making the world bright."

At the time, it had made perfect sense to me,

because I knew men could be gods. My father was surely a god, for he was the star around which my entire world revolved. I beheld his kingdom from atop his strong, broad shoulders. Up there, it was possible to witness things that would've otherwise gone unnoticed by one so small.

Standing in more or less the same spot fourteen years later, I wondered if knowing the truth—that Mason wasn't my real father—would've made a difference. Most likely not. When you're young, you'll accept almost anything as normal. And back then, Mason Black had been my everything.

Who the hell was I kidding? Long after he'd abandoned me at the age of twelve, he was still my everything.

I would have gladly gone to the grave believing he was my flesh and blood. It wasn't until a few weeks ago that I learned the truth about him, but the damage had already been done. He'd broken my heart into a thousand pieces by leaving me six years ago; what was a few hundred more?

Rising onto my toes, I craned my neck to scan the blockade of onlookers by the temple wall. Mason had warned me that weekends at the Met could be crowded, and crowded was an understatement. My bus arrived at Grand Central Terminal a few minutes after I was supposed to meet him in the lobby. By the time I joined a ticket line, I was already twenty minutes late.

I looked for him at the information kiosk, and when I didn't see him, I sent a text. Ten minutes and zero responses later, I headed into the Egyptian wing in the hopes that he'd gotten bored and gone inside without me.

That was half an hour ago.

Abandoning the temple, I took a seat on the stone lip beside the reflecting pool and pulled out my phone. No new messages. My foot took to bouncing; I was starting to freak out. It was possible Mason had left his phone at home, or forgotten to charge it. He probably thought I'd stood him up.

Or, far more likely, he hadn't shown up at all.

As far as I was aware, Mason had no idea I was privy to the fact that he wasn't my father. I was both dreading and anticipating his reaction when I confronted him about knowing the truth. Well, half the truth. I still didn't know who my real father was, only that Mason wasn't it. I hoped he might be able to shed some light on the subject, or at least be able to point me in the right direction so I could find him for myself.

But first, I had to find Mason.

With no other way to contact him and nowhere else to go, I was starting to get anxious. His address was unlisted. I didn't know anyone else in New York City, and the money in my bag wasn't enough to cover another bus ticket, plus food. There had to be an ATM somewhere in the museum. I'd hoped to save the bulk of my high-school graduation money, but if push came to shove, I supposed I could use some of it to rent a cheap hotel room or a bed at a youth hostel.

I was about to send Mason another text when I

5

heard an unmistakable gasp from the chorus of soccer moms idling nearby. I could almost smell their arousal.

The throng of women parted, and there he stood, daylight bursting through the clouds. I had to crane my neck a little to see all of him. He was taller than I remembered, and broader, his shirt hugging the muscles in his chest like a second skin.

My breath caught in my chest as I met his gaze. Mason was the sort of handsome that made people's necks snap as he passed, the kind you had to rub your eyes to believe. My mother used to say he didn't just make art, he was art. A walking, talking, living, breathing work of art.

He was the sun. It hurt to look at him.

"Hey Jetty," Mason said.

Smoothing my lychee-scented lip balm, I curtailed my grin into a modest smile.

"It's actually just Jett now," I said.

"Mind if I sit down, Just Jett?"

I smiled at his dad joke as he took a seat on the stone bench beside me. I was at a loss for words, but it didn't seem to matter. Mason's smile was as warm as midsummer, his hazel eyes tinged gold. Not a smirk of pretense or a squint of disenchantment to be found. Just wonder, pure and refreshing like a mouthful of ice water.

I swallowed, forcing my affection down. It was far too soon and six years too late to be thinking such thoughts about a man who had lied to me for over a decade and then disappeared without a trace. I may have come all the way from New Hampshire to see him, but I didn't want him to think this would be easy.

"Have you been here long?" I asked matter-of-factly.

"About an hour."

I winced. "Sorry. My bus was late. Didn't you get my texts?"

"I did." He scratched at the stubble along his jaw, drawing attention to his shirtsleeves. They'd been folded up to reveal the network of veins that snaked his arms like tributaries. I used to trace those veins with magic marker, all the way up to his shoulders, transforming his arm into a map of the Nile River.

"I decided to walk around in case you'd already come in," I said.

"I know. I watched you buy your ticket."

I leaned back to look at his face. "That was like, an hour ago."

He shrugged one shoulder. "I wanted to look at you."

My cheeks burned. As a rich and famous portrait artist, Mason had turned people-watching into a vocation. He used to draw me all the time when I was little, but just then I found his gaze unnerving, like the phantom sensation of having to pee before a performance. His scrutiny pared at my composure, and I was afraid he'd scrape away the layers only to be disappointed by what he found inside.

"See anything interesting?" I asked, keeping my tone light.

Mason cocked his head to study me. He seemed to be weighing his words. "Your hair's a lot darker than I remember. And you're taller, but that makes sense, considering how long it's been."

I wanted to ask him why it'd been so long. But he looked so pleased to see me, I didn't want to ruin the mood. I was already predicting an awkward conversation once I revealed my true motivations for this visit.

Mason and my mom had never married, but she'd given me his last name: Black. I have vague memories of him living with us when I was little, before the two of them broke up. Mason moved into his own apartment, and I spent nearly every weekend at his place, until the day he left. If I hadn't stumbled across a number in my mom's contacts, marked only with the letters *MB,* and sent a quick text from my own phone after downing one too many post-graduation tequila shots, he'd still be nothing but a memory.

"Your hair used to cover your ears," I said, still at a loss for any topic of substance. "It looks good short."

His mouth quirked up at the corners.

"So do you, Jett."

He nudged my arm and then waited, probably to see if I'd nudge him back. If I did, it would mean he could touch me.

I held my breath and nudged him.

Mason pulled me into a side hug, his big hand gently squeezing my shoulder. Pressed so close together, I couldn't help feeling comforted by his sturdiness and the pleasing scent of his clothes.

Over the next few hours we made our way through the American galleries, tethered it seemed by an invisible thread. I kept close, lured by the thrill of simply basking in his presence. Every now and then, he would pause to point out something about composition, or to shake the hand of yet another fan who recognized him as *the* Mason Black.

Rather than dine at one of the museum restaurants, Mason insisted I let him take me to his favorite Italian place with the good breadsticks. I could tell he was keeping a leisurely pace for my benefit, letting me soak in the sights and sounds and smells of the city. It'd been years since I'd visited Manhattan, and I missed it. Everything about it. The rush and the thrum and the weight of it.

The host at the restaurant recognized Mason and seated us at once. A few of the patrons eyed us curiously. I found the attention unnerving, but Mason appeared used to it. Not long ago, *Art in America* had dubbed him The Modern-day Egon Schiele for his contour line drawings of sex workers with their children. But the work that'd made him super famous was a series of frankly intimate paintings titled *The Family in Repose*: a father, mother, and their twin sons, cooking breakfast, clipping toenails, checking email, changing their socks. He'd lived with the family for two years, quietly observing.

Two years invested in a family that wasn't his own.

The host seated us at a quiet table in the back corner, away from prying eyes. Still, even the waiter seemed mildly starstruck as he took our orders. I couldn't blame him. When Mason's work started gaining traction a few years after he disappeared, I became obsessed. In place of concert posters on my walls, I had prints of Mason's paintings. Surrounding myself with his art allowed me to pretend he was still part of my life.

I followed his career with the zeal of a fangirl lusting after her favorite pop star. It was his genius that inspired me to pick up a paintbrush. As it turned out, I, too, had a knack for visual art—a knack that turned into a passion that led to an acceptance into New York University's studio art program.

Mason had been quick to jump on my thinly-veiled request for a trip into the city, going so far as to invite me to spend the summer painting in his private studio—an opportunity of a lifetime for any wannabe professional artist, but an even more monumental break for me. It was my chance to reconnect with the man whose love of art had rooted itself in me from the very beginning.

However, most importantly, it was my chance to get some answers about why he'd deceived me.

By the time our food arrived, piled high and piping hot, I was ravenous. He'd been right about the breadsticks. Over the next hour, we ate and talked about his works in progress and my plans for college. As eager as I was to confront him, I decided not to push for answers just yet. Whether it was pent-up resentment or the mystery surrounding Mason that made him seem so alluring, all I knew was that being around him made me feel needy in a way I wasn't used to.

"You still hate peas," he said, looking amused. I'd forgotten to ask for no peas in my gnocchi, and I was avoiding his gaze by pushing the little green globes around my plate. "Your mother always hated them, too."

"I know," I said. I suspected that was the reason she never forced me to eat them.

He pushed his own empty plate away. "How is Gretchen doing?"

It was strange, hearing my mother's name fall from his lips after all this time.

"She's good."

"Still seeing the podiatrist?"

I shook my head. "He's been gone for a while. The guy she's dating now is a complete corporate stooge."

"You don't like him?"

I shrugged. "He's nice, in a back-to-you-Tom sort of way."

"Does he wear themed ties?"

"Yeah, but he saves the really dorky ones for special occasions." It occurred to me that I couldn't recall ever seeing Mason in a tie. His style had always consisted of jeans and paint-stained tees with the occasional sweater. Today was no exception. "He's good to her, if that's what you're getting at."

"I'm more concerned with whether he's good to you."

"We tolerate each other." I tore off a hunk of garlic bread and swiped it through the sauce on my plate, cutting a clean line through the red. "So much curiosity about Mom's love life. You must miss her."

Mason didn't respond right away. "I'll always care about your mother."

I sensed his hesitation. "But?"

He shrugged. "But I'm sure I don't have to tell you she's guarded. It's hard being close to someone who hides so much of themselves from you."

Almost as hard as staying close to someone who disappears from your life altogether, I thought.

Still, I nodded in understanding. For as long as I could remember, my mother kept secrets, sometimes for no apparent reason. I knew next to nothing about her background, only that she'd had me when she was very young. Once, she let it slip that she'd grown up in a big, old house in Virginia with half a dozen bathrooms and twice as many fireplaces. When I asked if we could go see it someday, she immediately changed the subject.

"I'm the complete opposite," I said, freeing an elastic from my wrist. "Can't hold back to save my life, for better or worse."

"I'd say for the better."

His gaze tracked my fingers as I plaited my dark locks into a manageable braid.

"You're even more beautiful than I remember," he said.

Something like gratification trilled through me before I could tamp it down.

"Um, thanks."

The force of his stare and the intensity behind

it made my pulse stutter. For a brief moment, I imagined holding his fingers to my throat so he could feel the rampant beat.

"I hope that doesn't make you uncomfortable," he said. "You're stunning, and you've always been stunning. I have sketches I made of you as a child hanging in my studio. People ask me all the time, who's that gorgeous girl with the wide eyes? I tell them, that's my daughter. That's my little girl."

But I'm not his little girl, I thought, even as my arm hairs stood on end.

I'd always wondered what happened to those drawings, proof of all the times I had sat like a stone until my father's hand grew tired, no matter how bad my back ached or how numb my legs felt. I'd welcomed the suffering because I wanted him to look at me. For as long as he sketched me, I was the center of his universe. It was exhilarating, being on the receiving end of his concentration, like drunkenness, or falling in love.

Not that I had much experience with either.

"You look so much like Gretchen did at your age," he said, "only not as defensive. She's always been a granite wall, whereas you're translucent, like glass. You know how to let people in. There's beauty in that kind of openness. There's strength."

Though I knew Mason wasn't my father, I had to admit, it was easy to slip back into the role of the painter's daughter. Hearing him talk about my mother and our shared past, calling me his little girl, made me want to crawl onto his lap again. At the same time, it felt like trying to squeeze my feet into a cute pair of slippers that no longer fit.

"I miss sitting for you," I confessed, wondering if he missed sketching me. "Mom lets me draw her sometimes, but she fidgets."

"She always did." He studied me for a long moment. "She doesn't know you're here, does she?"

I stiffened. "She knows I'm in New York."

"But she doesn't know you're here to see me."

Funny, how the man who'd deceived me all those years could still make me feel guilty for lying to my mother.

When Mason and I began texting a few weeks ago, I still believed he was my father. One day, my mom saw his number flash across my phone, and in a flurry of tears and shouting, the likes of which I'd never seen from her before, she spluttered the truth: Mason wasn't my father, so there was no point in trying to reconnect with him—and no, she wasn't going to tell me who my real father was, no matter how hard I begged her.

Learning the truth just about shattered me all over again. I typed up a scathing message to Mason and came close to hitting send before I realized...if Mason had known my mother around the time she was pregnant with me, he might know something about my real father. At the very least, I wanted the chance to confront him in person about lying to me.

I still had every intention of confronting him today—assuming I could resist the temptation of slipping into old, familiar roles.

"She thinks I'm staying with friends," I said. "But it doesn't matter. I'm eighteen. I don't need her permission to visit you, or anyone."

Mason speared a piece of my cold gnocchi and brought it to his lips. His gaze never left me, not even as he chewed.

"She told you, didn't she?"

I blinked, frozen. "Told me what?"

"We've been sitting across from each other for almost two hours, and not once have you called me Dad. I have a hunch it's because you know the truth."

"Which is?"

His throat shifted as he swallowed. "I'm not your biological father."

There it was, the truth from the lying horse's mouth. I thought hearing him say it would feel vindicating, but all I felt was disheartened, and embarrassed at the tiny, vulnerable part of me that'd hoped it wasn't true.

"Why are you really here, Jetty?"

I had considered saving my interrogation for another day, but with the truth hanging in the air between us and the questions burning a pit in my stomach, I couldn't hold back.

"I want you to tell me who my real father is."

Chapter Two

❦

"I don't know who your father is," Mason said. "Gretchen never told me."

Bullshit. "You're telling me you agreed to raise some stranger's kid without knowing all the details first?"

He blinked slowly. "I didn't agree to raise a stranger's kid. I thought I was raising my own."

I winced at the flash of pain in his eyes. The possibility that my mother had lied to both of us had occurred to me, but I'd dismissed the notion outright. Frankly, it was easier to be mad at both of them.

"When did you find out I wasn't yours?"

"The night I took you out for ice cream after the movie. I thought Gretchen was going to chew me out for keeping you up on a school night... Turns out, she had other things to discuss."

I wished I could recall the details of that outing; if I'd known it would be our last, I'd have paid better attention.

I could only imagine how painful it must've been to discover the daughter he'd helped raise belonged to someone else. Still, it didn't justify his disappearing act after he'd been my father for twelve years.

"Is that why you left?" I asked. "Because you found out I wasn't really yours?"

His mouth tipped into a smirk. "I'm surprised Gretchen didn't tell you that part."

"Guess she thought it'd be better to make me spend my life wondering if it was something I did."

Mason's gaze softened. "No, Jett. None of it was ever your fault."

I studied his handsome yet guarded expression, growing more and more impatient. When he didn't move to elaborate, I pressed.

"Then, why did you go?"

He sighed heavily. "I'm sorry, but I can't say anything other than that it was the only thing I could do, given the circumstances."

"What does that even mean?"

"It means it's not my story to tell. Your mother's had a hard life, Jett. She doesn't like to talk about it, and I've done my best to respect that."

"What about my life? Do you think it's been easy for me, going through life thinking my father abandoned me?"

"No, I don't. And I'll go to the grave feeling sorry for the pain I caused you. But if Gretchen wanted you to know why, she'd have told you."

I couldn't believe I'd come all this way just to slam headfirst into a brick wall.

"But it *is* your story. Half of it, at least. Why can't you just tell me?"

"Because I made a promise, and I'm a man of my

word."

My chair creaked as I slumped against it. The sad, hurt little girl inside me shouted to keep pushing, keep arguing, but the finality in his tone made me bite my tongue. Whatever his reasons for leaving, he wasn't going to share them. I was used to this kind of withholding from my mother. I'd hoped Mason would be more forthcoming. No such luck.

"I know that's not the answer you hoped for," he said, "but it's the only one I can give you. Sometimes it's better to let the past stay buried."

Easy to say when you're the one who buried it, I thought.

Mason slid his hand across the table toward me.

"Jett, I can't tell you how sorry I am for taking off. You deserve an explanation, and it kills me that I can't give you one. I understand if you don't want to hear this, but I need you to know that, regardless of whether or not you're my daughter, I've never stopped loving you."

My stomach dropped into my Doc Martens. I didn't want to believe him. At the same time, I knew it was possible to love someone long after they'd disappeared. I wasn't sure how I could still love Mason after all the lies and missed birthdays and Christmases, but I did.

If I could love him after everything he'd missed, then perhaps it was possible that a part of him still loved me, too.

"Can you at least tell me where you've been, Mason?" Unlike the title Dad, his name felt awkward in my mouth, like a misshapen candy.

"I did some traveling after The Family series took off. But for the most part I've just been here in New York, working."

"Working so hard you couldn't find one free weekend to come see me? Or five spare minutes to make a call?"

"I know how it looks, Jett, but—"

"But you made a promise."

He slid his hand back to his side of the table.

"I did. And part of that promise involved keeping my distance."

"So, what the hell changed? Why is it okay for me to visit you now? Enlighten me, because I'm having a hard time understanding why you suddenly give a shit."

"I've always given a shit, Jett. My leaving didn't change that. What changed is that you're old enough to make your own decisions. You chose to come here. I think that should count for something, don't you?"

"I came because I want answers."

"And I've told you that I don't have any. None that I can give you. So, where does that leave you now?"

"On a bus back to New Hampshire, I guess."

"Sure, you could go home, work a boring summer job at The Burger Barn, keep pressing your mom for answers she'll never give you. Or, you could stay here. Spend the summer getting to know the city, let me introduce you to other artists and dealers. My studio is yours, if you want to use it. So is my guest room. It's got a beautiful view of the park."

"You think you can bribe me with fancy paints and a nice view?"

"They are very fancy paints, and it's a damn fine view."

His playful smile almost made me lose my cool, but I held firm. I wasn't going to give in just because he was offering me the world—though his world was the one where I longed to live.

"I don't expect you to forgive me today," he said. "I have no right to ask you for anything, but I can make you a promise. I'll never leave you again, Jett. Not unless you want me to."

"Why would I want you to?" The words slipped out before I could stop them, and I realized I'd just betrayed my position. I was angry and frustrated, but I wanted to stay with him, and he knew it.

He shrugged. I almost missed the wounded glint in his eye.

"You might prefer the memory of the father I was to the man in front of you."

I didn't know what to say to that, so I said nothing. Clearly, I hadn't really known him back then either.

Still, whatever we were to each other, then versus now, I had a choice to make. I could hold tight to my anger and buy myself a bus ticket home, closing the door on this new, mysterious Mason and his former role in my life forever. Or, I could accept his apology, allow him to make room for me in the world he'd built around himself, and spend the summer making up for lost time.

Unlike my mother, I'd never been very good at holding grudges.

"I don't know if I can get used to calling you Mason."

"So call me Dad—" His hazel eyes darkened as his mouth curved into another pulse-fluttering smile. "—or Daddy."

Chapter Three

As it turned out, this new, mysterious Mason owned two adjacent lofts on the top floor of a historic building in Manhattan.

We stepped out of the elevator into a white-walled corridor with two sets of double doors. He opened one set of doors and motioned for me to enter.

"My studio is across the hall," he said. "I do have some work to do in there later today. Think you can keep yourself busy for a few hours?"

I twirled in a circle, face turned up toward the exposed beams and copper piping. The living room was massive.

"I'm sure I'll manage." I squinted against the natural light streaming through the floor-to-ceiling windows. "So, this is how the other half lives."

"This is how *you* live for the next few months." He took my bag and slung it over his shoulder. "Come see your room."

I followed him upstairs to the loft and down the hall to a good-sized bedroom with brick walls and more natural light. He'd been right about the very nice view.

"Bathroom's down the hall," he said. "My room's just past that. Towels are in the closet at the end of the hall. Help yourself to anything in the fridge."

He set my bag on the bed and then showed me how to operate the electronic curtains in case I didn't want to wake up with the dawn. I sat on the bed and scanned the room, taking in the potted ferns on the windowsill, the linens in turquoise and violet. He'd remembered the color palette in my bedroom at the old house. The thought made me smile.

I stood as he turned to go.

"Dad?"

He paused in the doorway.

"Thank you for lunch," I said.

"You're welcome, sweetheart."

The epithet wrapped itself around my chest like ribbon, making it hard to breathe. I took a tentative step toward him. "Can I have a hug?"

Mason's eyes crinkled at the corners. "Of course."

He wrapped his arms around me, cupping the back of my head with his palm. I pressed my nose to his throat. He smelled good, like pine and cloves and peppermint, just as I remembered.

"I've missed you, too," he whispered into my hair.

I couldn't help chuckling at his mindreading abilities. I angled my mouth toward his cheek, intending to give him a quick peck. He must've had the same idea, because when I turned my face, our lips met.

The room held its breath. My eyes drifted shut as my fingers closed around his shirt collar. His stubble tickled my chin. Every inch of me tingled as tension gathered in my stomach, sliding low, then lower, between my legs.

A voice inside my head shouted, *stop*. This couldn't be happening. It had to be a misfire, bad wiring, mistaken identity. My thoughts sprinted alongside my pulse, trying to make sense of my misplaced desire.

Plenty of parents kiss their children on the mouth, I told myself. It wasn't inherently sexual. Mason hadn't been a father to me since I was twelve, but he'd played the role long enough that my body should've known better.

I drew back. Mason's eyes snapped open, taking in my darting gaze. Mortified, I let my feet carry me back to the bed where I forced my hands to start unpacking.

"Sorry," I said. "I didn't mean to... It was an accident."

When I could no longer stand the heat of his stare on my back, I spun to face him.

"Would you please say something—"

There was no one else in the room.

Chapter Four

My mind swam as I sat on the bed and touched my fingers to my lips. It was only a kiss. Accidental and embarrassing, sure, but it could've happened with anyone.

I needed to believe that.

The intercom buzzed in the living room. Mason's shoes thudded down the stairs. There came another buzz, the squeal and bang of the door as it opened and closed, then silence, loud and accusatory.

I sat there, unmoving, until I couldn't take the stillness any longer. With twitchy hands, I unpacked my toiletries and clothes before venturing out to explore the rest of the apartment.

Downstairs, the kitchen was fully stocked with food and flavored seltzer. I used to drink lemon and lime seltzer as a kid. I wondered if Mason had started drinking it after he left, or if he'd bought them just for my visit. I tried to watch TV but nothing held my interest.

I couldn't stop thinking about the kiss.

The sun was halfway to setting when I heard a woman's laughter on the other side of the door. Curious, I got up to investigate.

Easing the door open a couple of inches, I peered into the hall. Mason stood by the elevator, across from a dark-skinned woman with enviable curves. Her voice dripped with affection when she said his name.

Jealousy, sharp and inexplicable, flared in my gut. Mason was a handsome man, and she was obviously an attractive woman. Who was I to begrudge them a flirtation, or anything else?

I forced myself to return to the couch.

Mason sauntered in shortly after and sat in one of the recliners. I pretended to be riveted by the selection of on-demand movies.

"Sorry that took longer than expected," he said. "I'm starting a new piece and the planning always takes twice as long as the painting. I hope you weren't too bored."

"I'm fine." I fiddled with the volume settings and pleaded with my voice to sound less pained. "Who was she?"

"My model," he said. "Her name's Krista. I'll introduce you next time."

I looked at him and then had to look away. He was assessing me again, his gaze penetrating my strained veneer of calm.

"Are you hungry?" he asked.

"I could eat."

He rose from the chair. "I'll make us dinner."

Normally I would have offered to help, but I needed to maintain some distance, at least until

I'd forgotten about what happened in my bedroom. Thankfully, as we sat down to eat, Mason seemed content to pretend we had never kissed, which was fine by me.

After dinner, he asked me to show him some of my sketches. We spent the rest of the evening paging through my sketchbook, with Mason pointing out the drawings he liked and how I could improve others. I felt buoyant, high on validation. I'd almost forgotten about our kiss entirely, until his hand captured mine on the sofa and I felt a jolt like a spark in my chest.

I prayed he wouldn't notice my nipples stiffening beneath my shirt.

When he stopped at my door to say goodnight, he didn't cross the threshold. He simply asked if there was anything I needed.

"I'm all set," I said. "Thanks."

"My pleasure." He smiled warmly. "I love you, Jett. You don't have to say it back. I just want you to know."

The words nestled somewhere between my heart and my hips. I nodded, struggling against the full-body flush.

"Goodnight, sweetheart," he said.

"Night, Dad." I clasped my hands together to stop myself from reaching for him.

Chapter Five

Hours later, I still couldn't sleep, and it wasn't because of the unfamiliar bed or the sounds of the city drifting up from the streets below.

It was the kiss.

Every time I closed my eyes, I felt the smoothness of Mason's lips and the heat of his breath, the tickle of his short-cropped beard against the corners of my mouth.

The memory if it made me want to touch myself.

My feelings were beyond inappropriate, yet I couldn't deny the truth. The kiss had happened, and here in the dark on this borrowed bed, there was no pretending I hadn't liked it.

I tossed and turned, waiting for a wave of nausea to hit, for my skin to crawl, but all I felt was restlessness. Sleep was out of the question. I checked the time on my phone and found two missed calls from my mother. At just after twelve o'clock, it was too late to call back; I'd deal with her shit in the morning.

Exasperated, I climbed out of bed and pulled on a long T-shirt over my sports bra. I listened for signs that Mason might still be awake as I crept into the hall. Hearing nothing, I tiptoed downstairs to the kitchen.

Lights from other apartment buildings glittered in the distance. The moon was out in full, painting the floors in shades of gray and silver. I poured myself a glass of water and went to stand by the window. It was too bright out to see the stars, but the streetlights were a more than adequate replacement.

Brake lights flashed as traffic lights winked from red to green to yellow. This far above the ground, I couldn't help feeling like a fairytale princess locked in a tower, cut off from reality and time itself. Only no one had trapped me and I didn't need saving. I could leave any time I wished.

I padded back upstairs. Soft noises emanating from down the hall stopped me on the way to my door. After a moment's hesitation, I crept toward the source of the sound, all the way to Mason's bedroom.

His door had been pushed closed, but hadn't latched completely. I pressed my ear to the slab—too firmly. My heart stopped as the door inched open just enough for a curious eyeball to peer through.

Inside, I saw Mason seated with his back to the headboard, his face bathed in iridescent light. I heard another soft moan.

The flat-screen television wasn't visible from this angle, but the grunts and cries confirmed what I suspected: he was watching porn.

Only, he wasn't.

Porn might've been on the screen, but Mason's eyes were closed.

My body tensed with undue fascination.

He wore only a pair of black boxer briefs, his long legs stretched out across the enormous bed. I hadn't realized he'd been hiding a six pack under all those paint-stained tees.

Inching forward, I brought my eye closer to the cracked door. It felt wrong to spy on him like this, but I couldn't stop myself. Part of me wanted to climb into his lap like old times, to trace the slight bump on his nose and stroke the high points of his cheeks. I had spent the past six years wondering about his life without me, what he did with his free time, where he slept.

I would run back to my room in a second, but first I needed a glimpse into his private life. His chest rose and fell. I thought he might be sleeping, until his hand slid into his lap. He cupped himself through his boxers, and I saw it, pushing at the dark fabric.

He was hard.

I gasped. Eyes closed tight, he rubbed himself slowly, like a man with all the time in the world. My inner muscles clenched along with my stomach, my blood running hot and cold, curiosity versus confusion.

Mason my father versus Mason the man.

I licked my lips, incapable of tearing my gaze away from his bulge. This was wrong. I was wrong. Still, I desperately needed to know what he was hiding in there.

My first, last and only relationship had existed entirely online with a German guy I met on an art forum. I had never touched a cock, or seen one in the flesh instead of on a laptop or phone screen, but I knew firsthand how watching someone masturbate could be sexy under the right circumstances. I'd just never imagined those circumstances would involve me spying on the man who used to be my father.

I wanted to race back to my room almost as much as I wanted to stay and see more.

Mason pulled the waistband of his boxers down over his cock. I had always looked forward to this part with my ex, what I thought of as *the reveal.* But Mason's erection was an entirely different beast.

The damn thing was almost as thick as my wrist. It couldn't possibly fit inside a person.

Sweat trickled down from my hairline as I worked to control my breathing. Mason wrapped his hand around his cock and began to stroke. I clamped my lips together to hold back a whimper, and before I knew what'd come over me, I was reaching down to massage my pussy through my underwear.

I wasn't supposed to react this way toward the man who'd raised me. I wasn't supposed to feel what I felt watching his fist move up and down over his cock.

The tip glistened in the light from the television. He stopped pumping only to brush his thumb over the place where the head met the shaft. Lips parted, he choked out a grunt, then sucked air through his teeth.

Desire is a universal language; I didn't have to be fluent to speak it.

The look on Mason's face was a question to which

my body responded with a resounding yes. Slipping beneath the edge of my underwear, I aimed straight for my clit, which was pebble-hard and so sensitive that I nearly cried out when I touched it.

Setting the water glass down on the floor so I wouldn't drop it, I rubbed myself with one finger, then two, then one again when the pressure became too much. My pussy was sopping, and there seemed to be no end to how wet I could become. It felt right. It felt wrong. It felt so good that it felt bad until it inevitably felt good again.

Mason's head fell back against the headboard. He quickened his pace, gripping tightly and stroking all the way over the head and then down. Part of me wanted to pause and simply take it all in so I wouldn't miss anything, but there was no prying my hand away when I was so close—

When *we* were so close.

"Daddy..." I sighed the word, not sure where it had come from or why it had floated to the top of my mind at this exact moment. I hadn't called him Daddy since I was small enough to fit on his shoulders. It should've felt wrong, but there was no denying how much it turned me on to say it.

He tugged down on the base of his erection, as streaks of translucent white leapt onto his stomach. His jaw clenched. He pumped once, twice, three times, before finally letting go of his cock.

The clatter of his cellphone rattling on the bedside table jolted me back to my senses. I tore my hand from my underwear and released the breath I hadn't realized I was holding.

Mason scowled and picked up the phone.

"What?" he rasped. He hit a button on the TV remote, muting the sound, then tossed the remote control to the foot of the bed.

I started backtracking into the hall on trembling legs.

"Calm down, Gretchen, I can't understand you."

I stopped short. Why was my mother calling him so late at night? Reluctantly, I crept back toward the door, still swollen, still aching, still struggling to understand how my body could betray me like this.

He stared blankly ahead, squinted, then smirked.

"Well, where's she supposed to be?" he asked, his tone mocking. "You won't let me see her for six years and now you're calling because you've lost track of her?"

My breath stuttered on its way into my chest. The only response my mother had ever offered as to why he had stopped visiting was, *your father has his reasons.* Of course, I knew now that he wasn't my father, but even so, she'd been happy to let him pretend for over a decade. What could have happened to make her forbid him from coming to see me?

There was a long stretch of silence, followed by a heavy sigh.

"Yes, she's here," he said, and a cold splash of irritation washed over me. I'd already told him my whereabouts were none of her business.

Mason sat quietly. Whatever my mother had to say, she was taking a hell of a long time to say it.

"You're damn right, I invited her. Jett is old enough to make her own decisions... What's that supposed to mean? Look, whatever agreement we had about my role in her life ended on her eighteenth birthday. I'll assume you didn't bother to pass along that card either... For fuck's sake, you couldn't make something up? She thinks I abandoned her... I don't even know what to say to that."

He pinched the bridge of his nose.

"She was my daughter for twelve years," he continued. "I never should've let you force me out, and I'm sure as hell not sending her home. She's safe here..." His gaze hardened. "You know what? Go ahead. While you're at it, you can tell her how you got ahold of those password-protected emails."

He lobbed his phone at the foot of the bed. I stood like a statue, simmering with anger and confusion. My mother had lied to me; that was hardly a surprise, but the fact that she'd invaded my privacy made my blood boil. As for what Mason had said about her forcing him to leave, I hadn't even begun to process. What could've happened that was so dangerous my mother had insisted he cut me out of his life?

I came to the city looking for answers, only to end up with twice as many questions.

Mason scrubbed at his face with the hand he hadn't used to jerk off. He righted his boxers and rose from the bed. I realized he was probably on his way to the bathroom, which meant he'd open the door to find me standing there if I didn't move fast.

I scurried back to my room, praying he wouldn't

hear my footsteps.

Back in bed with the covers pulled up to my chin, I shut my eyes and listened for the pounding of footsteps. When they didn't come, I began to count. If Mason hadn't stormed in by the count of one hundred, I could assume he hadn't heard me.

At one hundred one, I rolled onto my back, my heart one rogue beat away from busting a hole through my chest.

Nothing I'd learned from the moment I arrived in the city made sense. I hugged myself and rocked from side to side as uncertainty, embarrassment, and arousal tumbled like gym shoes in the dryer that was my stomach.

I had kissed the man who was once my father and watched him jerk off. I'd invaded his privacy—like mother, like daughter. *Ha.* Worse, I had almost gotten off while watching him.

Even now, imagining him hard and flushed, was enough to make my clit throb. I could feel the wetness between my legs, soaking the crotch of my underwear.

Slowly, almost against my own will, I inched my fingers downward.

Eyes closed tight to hold back tears, I surrendered to the gush of pleasure, envisioning another set of fingers in place of my own. Strong fingers. Calloused fingers. Stained with paint and charcoal.

I came like a shot within seconds, fierce and penetrating, teeth gritted and toes curled.

Shifting onto my side, I rode the waves of my

orgasm. Panting and twitching. Soothing and stilling.

Footsteps approached, quiet and measured. My pulse thundered in my ears. Why hadn't I heard the doorknob click? I swore I'd closed it, but it's possible I'd forgotten to pull it shut in my rush to get back into bed. I kept still as a corpse, as the footsteps grew closer, stopping beside my bed.

Mason must've heard me after all, or worse: maybe he'd heard me fingering myself. My inner muscles tightened involuntarily at the thought. Then again, if he had heard me, he would've known I wasn't really sleeping. So, why was he just standing there? Perhaps he only wanted to check on me.

He lingered beside my bed for what felt like an eternity, then retreated. The door clicked shut.

Finally, I let myself breathe.

A car alarm blared somewhere in the city far below. Sirens wailed. I drifted, depleted and confounded, yet grateful to be above it all, in Mason's castle in the clouds—a place seemingly removed from reality. From consequence. From right and wrong.

I didn't see it until I opened my eyes the next morning.

On the nightstand, backlit by the rising sun: the glass of water from the night before.

The one I'd left outside his bedroom door.

Chapter Six

I was ten years old the first time I modeled for an artist who wasn't my father. At the time, Mason was teaching drawing and studio art at the local community college. He'd warily agreed to let me sit in on his evening classes, as long as I promised not to get in the way.

Some nights, he'd place a table in the center of the classroom and arrange it with cut flowers and fruit. Other nights, he'd bring in a model for figure drawing.

My favorite model was a dark-skinned woman named Nadia. She had thick eyebrows and a wine-red mole on her neck and crepe-papery stretch marks around her navel. I could've sketched her for hours and not captured everything there was to see on the landscape of her skin.

One evening, the model who was supposed to show up canceled at the last minute. My father appeared to take the news in stride, and quickly began searching the classroom for items he could use in a still life.

I can't explain it, but from the time I was very young, I was always deeply attuned to my father's moods. I wet the bed for weeks before he moved out of my mother's house, and peeled the skin around my fingernails bloody in the days before he left town for good. When he grew solemn, I cried. When his teeth clenched in anger, my stomach cramped.

That night in his classroom, I could feel the tension rolling off of him like storm clouds. I had to do something.

"Daddy," I said, hooking his sleeve. "I'll do it."

"Do what, Jetty?" He waved me off his arm.

"I'll sit for the class."

He started to shake his head no and then stopped, his gaze assessing. I stood up straighter to show him I meant business. After a long and thoughtful pause, he told me to take off my shoes and socks and go take a seat at the center of the room.

I had been my father's model for years, so I knew what was expected of me. What I didn't expect was the weight of all those stares. They bore down on me like one of those lead aprons they make you wear when you get an x-ray. I imagined myself sinking through the floor.

Mason kept a close eye on me, making sure I got enough bathroom breaks and time to stretch between poses. Eventually, I settled into the job, lulled by the scraping of pencils and buffing of erasers. I began to have fun with it, choosing complex postures that involved standing on one foot, or twisting myself into a human pretzel. I was a lanky kid, long-limbed and flexible. The best part was getting to walk around and survey the sketches afterward.

My father ended class twenty minutes early; he could tell I was getting tired. On their way out, students approached us to thank him for the opportunity to study such a lovely subject. Most children couldn't sit still for more than a few minutes, they said. I was a rare gem.

"You have a beautiful daughter," said a man with a talent for capturing hands and feet. "I hope we'll be seeing more of her." My father thanked the student with a proud smile.

"You did great tonight, Jetty," he said, as we were locking up the classroom. "Thanks for volunteering."

I danced and skipped all the way down to the parking garage.

Back home, I told my mother and her then-girlfriend how much fun I'd had posing for my father's class. My mom's face turned pale as she listened. Before I could finish telling her what the students had said about me, she rushed into the kitchen to call my father.

"What the hell were you thinking?" she hissed into the phone. "You know how I feel about Jett being photographed in public... I don't care that it's just a drawing, I don't want pictures of her floating around where anyone could see them."

My stomach braided into knots. I thought I'd done a good thing by offering to model for my father's class. His students had seemed happy. Had I done something wrong?

"Mason, if I find out you've brought her to another one of your classes, no man or god will be able to protect you, and you will never see her again."

By then, I knew better than to believe in ancient gods who drove magical chariots across the heavens, or that my parents were anything more than human. But it occurred to me that if my mother were a goddess, she would be a vengeful one.

Chapter Seven

I lay in bed staring at the glass of water until almost noon.

When my anxiety could no longer stand up to my hunger, I threw on a robe and padded down to the kitchen. There were muffins and jam waiting on the table, a fresh pot of coffee in the carafe, and a note about hardboiled eggs in the fridge. I munched a blueberry muffin and poured myself a mug of coffee. The brew was strong, just how I liked it, though there was no way Mason could've known.

After breakfast, I showered, hand-washed my bra and left it to dry in the bathroom. I'd packed light so I wouldn't have to check my bag at the museum. A few pairs of underwear and pants, some simple shirts. Whatever I could fit in my laptop bag. I put on a fresh tank and yesterday's jeans, which were clean enough, and made a mental note to ask Mason about the laundry situation—

As soon as I was able to look him in the face again.

My whole body knotted with embarrassment as memories from the previous night came rushing back. I had watched the man I once called Daddy jerk himself off, then eavesdropped on an illuminating phone call between him and my mother. To top it all off, I'd made myself come imagining his hand between my thighs.

It was beyond twisted. It was fucked up. But the worst part, without a doubt, was the possibly of him suspecting I'd stood captivated outside his bedroom door, watching him fuck his own fist. Whether or not he'd heard me touching myself afterward was still up for debate.

I sat on the edge of the bed, my thoughts racing as I tried to make sense of it all. Was I so desperate to rekindle Mason's affection toward me that I'd twisted my innocent curiosity into something perverted? Technically, he wasn't my real father, but he'd been my dad for twelve years—eighteen if you counted the time I'd spent in the dark. Then, there was the fact that Mason had kissed me—or I'd kissed him. Either way, lines had been blurred from the moment I set foot in his apartment. I wasn't his daughter anymore, but I was hardly a stranger.

I had no idea what we were to each other now.

Even if I tried not to think about what I'd witnessed, there was still the late-night phone call to consider. The information Mason had unwittingly revealed: my mother, believing I was in danger, had told my father to leave me, and he'd agreed to go.

As awkward as I felt, I was desperate for answers, and right now, Mason was the only person who could give them to me.

I found his studio unlocked and unoccupied. The

layout was identical to his apartment across the hall, but with less furniture. Four easels had been positioned around what would've been the living room, all facing a futon that sat open in the center, layered with green and blue cloth. A plastic bin filled with more colorful shrouds stood off to the side. Nearly every surface lay strewn with brushes, palette knives, and tubes of paint.

I walked the perimeter of the room. On the table closest to the wall of windows, I found Mason's sketchbook wedged beneath a set of canvas stretcher bars. Carefully, I freed the sketchpad and went to sit on the futon.

The first dozen or so pages contained sketches of random body parts: arms, hands, shoulders, calves. Some crossed out, others so faded they could've been made years ago.

I stopped flipping when I came across the model I'd seen him talking to in the hallway last night, splayed out on the futon, naked, with her hand between her legs.

"Whoa." My fingers twitched against the paper. I turned the page and there she was again on her stomach, then on her side. Pages upon pages of her masturbating in various poses.

My breath stalled. I didn't want to think about the circumstances surrounding these images. Apart from my suspicion that this woman had to be more than just a model to him, seeing the drawings only served to remind me how badly I missed being his muse.

Not that I'd ever posed for him like this. Not that

I'd wanted to...

The door swung open and Mason stepped inside. He wore jeans and a green T-shirt that brought out the green in his eyes. His calm wavered for the briefest of moments when he saw me.

"Hey." He smiled. "When did you get up?"

"A while ago." My pulse kicked into overdrive. "Thanks for breakfast."

"Did you see my note about the eggs? You should eat some protein with your muffins. I don't want to send you off to college malnourished."

"I'll have two for lunch," I said, more than a little touched by his concern for my health.

He set the plastic bag he'd been carrying onto the counter by the sink, then proceeded to unload the contents—chalk, in various colors by the look of it.

I tapped my finger nervously against the sketch-book in my lap, struggling to come up with a natural way to talk about last night's phone call.

"Your mom called last night," he said, beating me to the punch. He turned his back on the sink, the heels of his hands braced against the countertop. "She knows you're here."

I feigned surprise. "How?"

"Apparently she called your friends." If Mason wanted to confront me about eavesdropping or spying on him, it was now or never.

A few seconds passed.

"Did she say anything else?" I asked when the silence became deafening.

"She's not happy you lied about where you were

going."

I had to laugh. "How very pot-meet-kettle."

"She just wants to know that you're safe."

"Well, I am. Aren't I?" I flipped to a different page and struggled to keep my expression neutral while staring at a pencil rendition of a vagina with two fingers in it.

I felt Mason's gaze like a hand gliding down my arm to the image in question. He cleared his throat. "You know, sketchbooks are kind of like journals. You shouldn't go through them without the artist's permission."

"Sorry." I closed the book. "I just wanted to see what you've been working on."

He lifted the sketchbook from my lap. "Krista's supposed to come by for a session this afternoon. I'll let you stay and watch if she's comfortable with it."

"I'd like that," I said, curiosity overriding my jealousy. "Is she your girlfriend?"

"Who, Krista?"

I nodded.

"I don't have a girlfriend."

Mason returned to the sink to get a glass of water.

All at once, my curiosity condensed to a stone in my throat.

"Dad, I'm sor—"

"I should give you a tour of the studio," he said, cutting me off. "The sooner you're familiar with the space, the faster you can make use of it."

He offered me the glass he'd just filled. I took it, meeting his gaze over the rim.

All at once, a current of understanding passed between us. He wasn't going to ask about what I'd seen or heard last night. In return, he wouldn't mention the glass or how it wound up in my room. I could keep my dignity and my place in his home for the summer. All I had to do was commit to an unspoken truce: I saw nothing. I heard nothing. There was nothing to discuss.

As he must've suspected, my embarrassment over what I'd seen was rapidly eclipsing my immediate need to know the details of his late-night phone call.

Closing my eyes, I tipped the water into my mouth and swallowed.

Mason's studio was unlike any classroom I'd ever worked in. He had all the best-quality paints and more brushes than an artist could ever use in a lifetime. He gave me a spot at his drawing table and my own easel, and permission to experiment with whatever tools and supplies sparked my interest. If I'd ever doubted the authenticity of his interest in my art, his encouragement and willingness to share his workspace killed it dead.

I parked myself in front of the window with a massive sketchpad and some charcoal and started drawing clouds. That was my favorite way to warm up. No matter how hard you tried, you couldn't fuck up clouds. You could only make them stormier.

"You pout your lips when you draw," he said.

"Do I?" I asked, not the least bit self-conscious now that I was in my element.

Mason, seated in a nearby chair, had been watching me work for almost an hour in comfortable silence. He shifted, the motion making the chair squeak. "Your mom used to do the same thing. Must be genetic."

That made me pause. "I didn't know Mom could draw."

"She preferred photography. You were her favorite subject. We were constantly stepping on each other's toes. Me with my sketchpad, her with her Nikon."

"She never told me she took photos," I said, not that I was surprised. Every secret talent was just another piece to the mysterious puzzle that was my mother. I resumed dragging a charcoal-stained finger along the underside of a foreboding cumulonimbus.

"Your mom had a knack for capturing nature. I prefer people. All the little private rituals we perform when we think no one's watching."

"I know." I met his gaze. "I've been following your work for years."

His smile betrayed a twinge of sadness.

A soft buzz disrupted the quiet that had settled between us. Mason drew his phone from his pocket, thumbed at it, then frowned.

"Well, shit."

"What's wrong?" I asked.

"Krista has the flu." His chest rose and fell with a heavy sigh. "This is going to set me back."

I laid the sketchbook on the floor. "Can't you find someone else?"

"Sure, but that would take a few days at least.

I was hoping to finish the preliminary sketches this afternoon."

An idea surfaced like a bottle in the ocean, a message borne from the deep.

"I could do it," I said.

He took in my face, my posture, my folded legs, then shook his head.

"Thank you, but that won't be necessary."

"It's not like I don't have experience," I said. "Come on, it'll be like old times."

"This is different," he said, his gaze hardening.

Technically, he was right. I'd seen the conceptual drawings in his sketchbook. This project was inherently sexual. He was trying to turn an intimate moment inside out, to take the most private activity in which a person could partake and make it public. If I did this, I would be laying myself bare for his and everyone else's perusal.

The thought of it scared and excited me. It made my toes curl.

"Dad, you're letting me work in your studio and stay in this incredible apartment for free. Let me do this for you."

"You're here as my guest, Jett, not as a tenant. You don't owe me rent or favors."

"It's not a favor." The offer was as much for my benefit as it was for his. Maybe more so. "I want to do it."

Mason scrubbed his jaw, his expression dubious. The chair creaked as he stood. He crossed the room and entered the walk-in supply closet, then brought out a blue terrycloth robe.

He presented the robe to me, his stare daring me to flinch.

"You can change in the bathroom."

I took the robe and rose from my chair. I was halfway to the bathroom when I heard him say, "You don't have to do this, Jett. I can find someone else."

I stopped. The words resounded in my ears, deafening. He could find someone else. Anyone else. Like he had scores of hopefuls lined up around the block, desperate to model for him. Like I was replaceable.

He hadn't meant it that way, but that's how it felt.

I draped the robe over a stool. He offered a kind smile, like he'd anticipated me changing my mind.

Grasping the hem of my tank top, I pulled my shirt off right there in front of him.

Mason's eyes rounded with stark surprise. Letting my shirt fall to the floor, I unzipped my jeans and shucked them along with my underwear. I stood naked before him, hips squared and shoulders pulled back to accentuate breasts that stood quite proudly on their own.

A breath fell from Mason's lips as his gaze caressed me. Goose bumps skittered along my arms and legs. The man could've wrapped me in burlap and it wouldn't have made a damn bit of difference. As far as most of the world knew, I was Mason Black's daughter. I had his name as well as his love.

He couldn't replace me.

"We're going to need a lot of black." He reached into the bin overflowing with fabric and proceeded to pull out yards and yards of midnight-colored cloth.

Chapter Eight

I waited as Mason readied the scene, my nipples gathering to points in the cool air of the studio. He stripped the futon, replacing the vibrant fabrics with the darker ones he'd selected.

"Too much color detracts," he said, though it wasn't clear if he was talking to himself or to me. "You don't need color. Just light. Lots of light." He arranged the materials, scrunching some pieces and smoothing others. He raised the shades on two of the windows, then turned to me.

"Have a seat," he said, gesturing to the futon.

Breathing deeply to temper the nerves I didn't want him to see, I lowered myself onto the tangle of fabric.

Mason circled the futon, then stopped in front of me, tall as a mountain. He'd shifted into artist mode, eyes tuned to the finer details, as he compared and contrasted what was in front of him with the image in his mind's eye.

"Pull your knees up to your chest," he said, and I did. "Cross your ankles. Good. Hold them."

He swept a lock of hair behind my ear, and I fought

the urge to lean into his touch like a cat. He tipped my chin up, then down, then he took a step back, arms folded.

"Lie on your back," he said.

Slowly, I eased onto the futon but kept my ankles crossed. My breasts splayed slightly to either side of my ribcage as my heart pounded against my sternum. I studied the ceiling and its highways of exposed beams and piping to distract myself from my nerves, listening for the sound of Mason's footsteps as he moved around the room.

"Slide your foot out," he said. "No, the other one."

His face hovered into view as he knelt on the mattress.

"I'll do it," he said. "Just relax."

His hand circled my ankle. My breath stuttered. Carefully, he drew my right leg out straight. My skin had never felt so sensitive, so conscious of its placement in relation to everything around it. He positioned me, guiding my limbs to where he wanted them to go. I closed my eyes, letting his adjustments lull me into a state of suspended detachment. I was a marionette with nerve endings for strings, and the man I had once called my father conducted the show.

He brushed my nipple in the process of draping my arm across my chest. I gasped at the jolt of pleasure that echoed in my hips.

"You okay?" He pressed a hand to my stomach.

I nodded yes, though I was far from okay. I was on fire, in spite of the gooseflesh that pricked across my skin as though I were cold. I was a tangle of string, threads of embarrassment and arousal and a yearning to be made and unmade by this man, this maker of beautiful things.

Mason turned his attention to the fabric around my shoulders, and I used his distraction to restore my mask of calm. The skin on my stomach was still warm from where his hand had been. I inhaled deeply, filling my head with the scent of chalk and paper, paints and thinner—comforting smells, classroom smells.

Without warning, he grasped my ankles, bent my knees, and spread my legs.

Last night's fantasies that felt far too much like memories flashed across my mind: the image of my father's hands gliding down to stroke my clit.

A whimper caught in my throat as his very real fingers parted my pussy lips, exposing me to the air.

I couldn't breathe, couldn't think. I was unmasked.

"Beautiful." He exhaled the word, his gaze centered between my thighs.

Heat rushed to my face. I flinched at the sense of loss I felt as he withdrew, my clit throbbing in time with my rampant pulse. He guided my arm by the wrist, resting my palm over my mound, then left to gather his supplies.

"I know this is awkward for you," he said, dragging a chair closer to the futon, "but I want you to touch yourself just like you would if you were alone. You can close your eyes if it helps."

I didn't know if it would help, but there was no way I could touch myself *and* look at him without having a nervous breakdown. My eyelids fluttered shut. I listened to the pounding of my heart, felt the throbbing of my pulse in my throat.

He didn't rush me. He didn't sigh or tap his feet.

Still, I could feel the minutes stretching like over-tuned guitar strings. When they snapped, would he send me out? Hand me my clothes like a pink slip and say, *Nice try, kid?*

The first time I masturbated for my ex over web-cam, I almost couldn't come. I was afraid of making weird faces or funny sounds. When I realized how quickly all of that faded into the background as soon as I began to touch myself, I was able to relax and let go. My arousal was sexy. My staccato moans and clenched teeth, the light from the screen reflecting off my slick fingers.

I began to draw small, imperceptible circles over my clit with my fingers. Wracking my brain for a fantasy, I reached for handsome celebrities, cute boys from school, chance encounters with sexy, mysterious strangers.

Knowing Mason was there and that he was watching made it hard to concentrate on anything else. It wasn't until I pictured the man himself tossing down the sketchbook and coming to kneel on the bed that my body started to respond.

I imagined him climbing over me, bending to take my nipple into his mouth. I saw him slide his tongue down to my circling fingers, where I spread my lips and let him kiss my clit, just like he'd kissed my mouth.

Groping for my breast, I rolled my nipple between my thumb and forefinger, then dipped the first two fingers of my other hand the slightest bit inside me to wet them. I was sopping, embarrassingly so.

Somehow, the knowledge that Mason had a front-row seat to my shame only made it hotter. I pretended my slick fingers were his tongue, that the hand around my breast was attached to his arm.

My legs trembled. My lips parted. I moaned.

Daddy...

"Stop," he rasped, his voice like honeycomb dipped in gravel.

My eyelids floated open and my fingers stilled. I glanced at him. He squeezed the arms of the chair, knuckles glowing white, his gaze scalding.

The look on his face was not unlike the one I'd seen him don last night, lustful and penetrating. I could still picture him with his cock in his hand. The thought sent a rush of molten pleasure through my veins.

"Stay just like that."

He flipped to a fresh page in his sketchbook and began drawing.

I lay still, my heart thumping in my clitoris as it pulsed against my fingers.

Nothing about this was normal. What we were doing, or how it made me feel. But I couldn't shake the feeling that I was finally where I belonged.

He drew me for forty minutes before he laid his pencil down, shaking his hand and flexing his fingers.

"Do you need a break?" he asked.

My limbs prickled from lying in the same position for so long. "Maybe a short one."

"We'll take ten," he said.

I wondered if I would have to touch myself again when we resumed, not that it would take much to get me going. I was still humming like an engine left to idle, easily revved to life.

Mason uncrossed his legs, resting both feet on the ground. His sketchbook slid to the side. I sat up to stretch and caught sight of what looked like the ridge of an erection braced against his thigh through his jeans.

I sucked in a quick breath and my inner muscles tightened.

How long had he been aroused? A few minutes? Since he'd spread my legs? Since I started touching myself?

I flicked my gaze away. When I looked up at his face, he was eyeing me as though he knew exactly what I'd seen—and wasn't sure how he felt about my seeing it.

His fingers flexed. For a second, I thought he might reach for me. He stood, and the way he positioned his sketchbook over his lap did not escape my notice.

"That's enough for today," he said.

With long, swift strides, he crossed the room and ascended the stairs to the loft, leaving me alone in the studio.

Chapter Nine

The air turned brittle in the sudden quiet, save for my heart beating like a drum in my chest. I donned the robe he'd tried to give me earlier, securing the terry-cloth sash around my waist, then padded to the sink for a glass of water.

I had wanted Mason to draw me like he used to. I should've known that it wouldn't be that simple.

Time had changed us. I wasn't his little girl anymore, and the things he wanted from his models were things I had no business giving him. It was natural for him to get aroused with the others. I wondered if he slept with them, too. The thought made me sick, not from disgust, but from jealousy.

I had never felt so emotionally naked with a boy before, let alone a man—and that's what Mason was, a man. Jagged and smooth, hard and soft, so many amazing things at once. Once upon a time, I was his daughter, and now I was a woman, with breasts and hips and the ability to give and receive pleasure.

He'd touched my pussy. No hand but mine had ever touched me there.

It happened so quickly I hadn't had time to process. But thinking about it now made me want to rub my thighs together.

I liked it. More than that, I wanted it to happen again.

Something was seriously wrong with me.

I refilled the glass, running the tap too hard and splashing water everywhere. I forced myself to drink, to drown, to suppress these chilling urges.

This man had abandoned me, but until a few weeks ago, he was still my father. Had six years apart turned us into strangers who could mistake one another for love interests? My mind cried out for an explanation for which my body had no answer. None that made sense, anyway.

My lungs begged for air. I coughed, water spluttering from my mouth into the sink. I moved to set the glass on the countertop and misjudged the edge. The glass fell to the hardwood floor and shattered.

"Fuck." I wiped my mouth with the back of my hand and stooped to gather the pieces.

Footsteps sounded on the stairs.

"What happened?" Mason asked, coming to stand behind me.

"I dropped a glass." My voice cracked from coughing. I couldn't look at him. "I'm sorry."

"Don't worry about it." He ripped a handful of paper towels from the roll under the cupboard and knelt to help me collect the pieces. "Careful. Don't use your bare hands."

"I'm fine." I sidestepped to toss the pieces into the trash. Pain shot through the base of my right foot.

PRETTY, DARK AND DIRTY

I shouted.

"Did you cut yourself?" Mason asked.

"My heel." I stood on one foot, afraid to put pressure on the wound.

He grabbed another bunch of paper towels, scooped me into his arms, and carried me to the futon like I weighed nothing.

"Hold these under your heel," he said, handing me the paper towels.

I saw the inch-long chunk of glass sticking out of my foot and winced. Mason returned to the sink, crunching glass beneath his thick-soled boots, and pulled a first aid kit from the cupboard. He dragged the chair he'd been sketching from over to the futon and rested my foot in his lap.

"You might want to bite down on something." He withdrew a pair of tweezers from the kit.

I closed my eyes and leaned back onto my elbows. A jolt of pain pierced my calf as he worked to free the chunk of glass from my flesh. I swore, then clenched my teeth against the throbbing in my foot.

"It doesn't look deep," he said. Something cold and wet that stung like the fire of a thousand suns slid over my heel. "Try to hold still."

"Sorry. It hurts so bad." I opened my eyes and a flood of longing filled my chest like oxygen. Memories of my father soothing my bumps and bruises, bandaging paper cuts.

He curved a hand over my ankle as he cleaned the wound; I tried not to think about where those fingers had been. He dabbed a glob of antiseptic, cool and tacky, onto the cut, then layered the area with gauze and secured the dressing with medical tape.

"You should stay off your foot for the next day or two," he said. "I'll help you into the apartment."

He held out his hand. I inhaled a ragged breath and accepted his help.

"Thanks," I said, wrapping my arm around his shoulders as he lifted me. "Good thing you weren't planning on having me stand for the painting."

Mason stayed quiet as we made our way to the door. "I've changed my mind about that, Jett. I don't think it's a good idea to have you model for me."

"Oh," I said, the word *why* sticking like a lump in my throat.

I should've been grateful. I should've been relieved. But all I felt was disappointment, like he was abandoning me all over again.

"Is it…" I couldn't make myself say the words, *is it because I made you hard?* "Did I do something wrong?"

"No. You were perfect." He let us into the apartment. "I shouldn't have asked you to do that."

"But I offered."

"It doesn't matter." He lowered me onto the couch cushion. "Anyway, it's better for you if you're not involved in my work."

"Better for me how?"

"Too much controversy."

"Since when are you shy about controversy?"

Mason pushed the ottoman closer so I could rest my foot on it. "I'm not. But it wouldn't fall solely on me. It would mark your career before it even started.

Better they see you as an artist first, and as my daughter second. Not as my subject."

"Who's they?"

"Critics, dealers, other artists."

"But I don't care how *they* see me." I couldn't believe I was fighting him on this, considering how badly the session had rattled me. But when the alternative was moving out of Mason's light and back to the darkness... I couldn't let that happen.

I couldn't have cared less whether the piece went viral, or never amounted to anything more than kindling. I could not handle losing him again.

"Dad, I'm doing this for you, not for them."

"I thought you were doing it for you."

"I am. I'm doing it for both of us."

"You're not hearing me, Jett." Mason rubbed his eyes. "I'm not going to paint you."

"Because you're worried about my career prospects?"

"Because you're mine." The edge in his voice told me not to push, but there was something in the way he said the word *mine* that hooked its claws in me. A twinge of anguish, the threat of darkness buried, something protective about his straight-backed stance.

No, not just protective.

Possessive.

Maybe there was a reason Mason had turned his mouth toward mine yesterday, the same reason he'd chosen not to confront me about spying on him. What if, when he spread my legs and touched my pussy and got hard watching me masturbate, it wasn't just a biological response?

I had spent the last twenty-four hours wondering if I was going crazy, when perhaps the truth lay somewhere on the ground between us.

Like the apple that never falls far from the tree.

"The kiss," I said, gazing up at him. "It wasn't an accident, was it?"

Mason eyed me like he would a predator, like I was something dangerous. Maybe I was. He shook his head no.

"Then this is real, what I'm feeling? It's not just in my head?"

"Only you know what you're feeling," he said. "But no, it's not all in your head."

I brought my fingers to my lips. Now that the pain in my foot had subsided, all I could think about was the fact that the man I'd called Daddy had wanted to kiss me. Not on the cheek or the forehead. On the mouth. Like a lover.

This attraction, this completely inappropriate desire I was battling, wasn't one-sided. Mason wanted this as much as I did. Wanted it so badly he hadn't been able to stop himself from kissing me, touching me, watching me.

A current of arousal quivered up my spine, making my skin tingle and my inner muscles clench. I was turned on again—and confused and conflicted. But still...

"I'm sorry, Jett," he said. "I didn't know it would be like this. I never thought I wouldn't be able to control myself, especially around you. But you don't have to worry. I'm not going to touch you again... or ask you to sit for me. I'll keep my distance, let you have the run of the house and the studio. I'll even leave the apartment, if it'd make you more comfortable."

I didn't want him to leave. I didn't want to stop sitting for him either, and I sure as hell didn't want him to keep his distance. I wanted him to pull me close, run his fingers through my hair, and then kiss me for real. A kiss with the power to turn back the clock and make me forget he'd ever left me.

"What if I don't want any of that?" I asked.

His expression shuttered. "Then I'll drive you to the airport and get you a first-class ticket home."

"That's not what I want either."

He held out his hands. "Tell me what to do here, Jett, and I'll do it."

My thoughts raced like frenzied kittens around in my head. For the life of me, I couldn't drum up the words to tell him what I needed, all the things I wanted him to do to me.

Shameful things. Unspeakable things. Nasty, dirty, forbidden things.

Fortunately, some languages are universal.

I untied the sash around my waist and opened the robe, letting it slide off my shoulders. Mason's gaze dipped to my breasts, the look on his face equal parts apprehension and arousal.

His lips parted. "Jetty?"

Hands trembling, I reached for him, my fingers closing around the fabric of his shirt. I drew him toward me, down onto the couch.

Before I had a chance to overthink anything, I swung my leg across his lap and straddled him.

"Kiss me again," I whispered.

I tipped my face and wetted my mouth...and waited.

Chapter Ten

The man who was once my father stared at me, unblinking, then cradled my face in his big, warm hands. He pressed his lips to mine. This wasn't a chaste kiss, like the one he'd initiated in my bedroom. This was slow and deliberate sensory overload.

I melted, letting the robe fall from my arms to pool around my hips.

Tension wound tighter and tighter between my legs. I touched his chest; his heart was rioting like a caged animal. I shivered and he must've felt it because within seconds his hands were on me, dispersing their warmth across my goose-prickled skin. Like his kiss, his touch was measured yet adamant, as though he feared he'd hurt me if he pressed too hard.

"I can't believe you're really here." He held my waist, then slid his palms to the small of my back.

I whimpered against his mouth. "Believe it."

He pulled me close, trailing kisses along my jaw. His stubble tickled my cheek and I laughed. I pushed my breasts against him, and the rumble in his chest rattled my body like a small seismic shift. He drew back to look at me.

"I want you, Jett. I know it's fucked up but no matter how hard I try, I can't get the thought of you touching yourself out of my head. But you have to tell me what *you* want."

I closed my eyes as he stroked my arms, his touch feather-light. In that moment there was no question in my mind—or in my body.

"I want this," I said. "I want you."

He kissed me, sliding his hands beneath the robe to grip my backside. I rocked against him, gasping when I felt the bulge of his erection against my inner thigh. The man who'd helped raise me was hard and there was no mistaking the cause. It was me.

"My God, how are you so beautiful?" he whispered between kisses. "And soft. You're so fucking soft."

I couldn't remember the last time I'd smiled like this, my top and bottom teeth bared, eyelids pinched, blurred vision.

Mason's tongue skimmed my bottom lip, a clear signal that he wanted to taste me. I offered my mouth and he delved inside, drawing a moan from deep in my throat. His tongue was warm and tasted of spearmint and black tea. I followed his lead, mimicking each nip and lick. This wasn't my first French kiss, but I was dreadfully out of practice.

He tugged his shirt off in one fluid motion and pulled me flush against him, flooding my chest and belly with heat, as his cock continued to demand attention—despite the confines of his pants. I wanted to see it, to hold it in my hands, but I couldn't make myself reach for it. What if I stroked too hard or not hard enough? There'd be no hiding my inexperience.

I groaned softly as he palmed my breasts, his thumbs raking over my nipples. Greedily, he took a puckered tip into his warm, wet mouth.

"Your nipples are luscious," he said. "I can't wait to taste every inch of you."

I moaned and clenched my inner muscles at the thought of him putting his mouth on other places, especially my clit. He pushed my breasts together, gliding his tongue back and forth over my nipples.

My fingers twitched, restless. I weaved them into his hair. Mason was making me feel amazing, but what the hell was I doing for him? His cock was there, begging to be touched, and I was too damn scared to do anything about it.

His gaze caught mine. "You okay?"

I nodded. "I'm fine."

"Just fine?"

I kissed him so he couldn't look at me.

"More than fine," I whispered.

Goddamn, those hands. They were everywhere—gliding up my back, down my chest, over my breasts and belly, between my legs. His fingers grazed my folds and I shivered, whimpering around our tongues, unable to keep my hips from rocking. He pressed the heel of his hand against me, putting pressure on my clit. His palm fit my mound like they'd been made for each other, like he'd sculpted me from clay to be his perfect match. I gave myself over to it, to him. I was his, and my heart swelled with gratitude for the fact that he seemed to want me every bit as much.

Mason dipped two fingers between my folds and spread my own moisture over my clit, drawing circles that made my calves and other, more intimate areas, spasm. My nails etched into his shoulders, but he either didn't notice or didn't care. His erection continued to prod my thigh, a reminder of all the things I should've been doing to him.

"I want..." I whined softly. "I can't..."

"Yeah, sweetheart?"

Hearing him call me sweetheart made my eyes burn with unshed tears. "I want to touch you."

"You are touching me."

"But..." I leaned my head on his shoulder, my thoughts coming at me in illicit pictures rather than words. "I want...more."

He smoothed my hair as a tender smile touched his lips.

"Where do you want to touch me, Jetty?"

I wanted to touch him where he'd touched me and everywhere else, to memorize the constellation of freckles on his chest and back. I wanted to know him better than he knew himself, to taste his elbows and the backs of his knees.

He placed my hands on either side of his face.

"Start here."

His fingers returned to my clit. Meanwhile, I made it my mission to learn more about this man I used to know so well.

I skimmed his cheekbones and brows, traced the edge of his jaw. I licked the pulse points below his ears, and kissed his collar bones, the hollow of his throat, his tight, tan nipples. I mapped him, this artist who had helped craft me, raking my fingernails down his chest and outlining the veins along his arm with my tongue.

Everything I wanted to do to him, I did.

Finally, I reached his belt buckle. With feigned confidence, I freed the leather strap from its metal enclosure and unfastened his jeans.

He sucked in a breath as I pulled at the front of his boxers, granting me access to all of him. I encircled his cock with all five of my fingers, my hand warmed by the blood-hot burn of his skin.

Mason watched intently, his eyes crescent moons, as I slid my fist along his length the way I'd watched him do it. Touching a cock, holding it firmly, was new to me. I couldn't believe how hard and soft it was. Such silkiness, on top of all that pressure.

After a few test strokes, Mason sighed and angled his pelvis toward me. I wrapped both hands around him, one above the other, and stroked down. He inhaled sharply.

"Was that good or bad?" I asked.

He chuckled breathlessly. "That was very good, sweetheart."

A smile consumed my face. He cupped my pussy with his whole hand—a simple gesture that made me feel cared for, comforted. He showed me how to round the head of his cock with every pass, how tight to squeeze the shaft without hurting him. I studied his reactions and adjusted my technique accordingly, captivated by how good I could make him feel using just my hands.

A cry bubbled up from my chest as he pushed two fingers inside me. I winced. The pain was brief, but sharp and unexpected.

"Did I hurt you?"

"A little," I said.

He stilled his hand and looked at me—*really* looked at me. "Jett, have you done anything like this before?"

Was my lack of experience that obvious? I shook my head, letting my hair fall over my face.

How was it possible to feel both eight and eighteen in the exact same moment?

Mason sighed and pressed his forehead to mine. "I wish you'd told me. I would've gone slower."

But I didn't want to slow down. Slowing down meant thinking, and thinking meant overthinking. Second-guessing. "Does this mean we have to stop?"

He planted a kiss between my eyebrows. I bristled at the tenderness in his touch, afraid he'd gone back to seeing me as just his little girl.

"I doubt we could stop ourselves even if we wanted to," he said with a teasing smile. "What do you think?"

I breathed a sigh of relief. "I don't want to stop. I want to make you come."

A deep, throaty growl rose from his chest.

"You first, Jetty." He kissed my neck and began sliding his finger in and out of me. His hands were big, his fingers thicker and longer than mine, allowing him to reach all the tender places I couldn't.

The pad of his thumb circled my clit. I humped his hand in tandem with pumping his cock. I couldn't help myself. It felt too damn good not to. He added a third finger and I flinched at the sting, stroking him faster to distract myself.

After a moment, the pain subsided and all I could feel was the tension and pleasure as he moved inside me, his thumb strumming my clit.

I tucked my face into the curve of his neck. He was going to make me come. The man who had taught me how to ride a bicycle was teaching me something far more important now: how to give and receive pleasure. He was going to make me come. The thought had my thighs shaking, my hands faltering in their rhythm.

"Are you close?"

"Uh-huh," I said. "Are you?"

"Don't worry about me, sweetheart. I could come just from listening to you."

He wrapped his other hand around mine on his cock. I let him glide my fist along his length and closed my eyes to concentrate on what he was doing to me. I pressed my nose to the skin of his throat. He smelled like home.

Eyes squeezed shut, I could almost see my orgasm waiting for me over my inner horizon.

"Don't stop," I begged. "Don't..."

"Not a chance, baby girl."

Baby girl. The epithet swaddled me like a security blanket. I felt warm all over, flushed from head to toe.

It struck me as a cruel joke that the man I was

forbidden from touching would also be the man who made me feel so treasured, so precious—the way a father should. It didn't matter that Mason and I weren't related by blood. He was my daddy. Now that I'd found him, I refused to let him go.

I met his thrusts with my own, rocking my hips in time with his fingers.

"Daddy?" I never thought I'd be the type to get off on baby talk, but straddling my long-lost father's lap with his fingers inside me, those were the only words that seemed to fit.

His cock throbbed in my palm. "Yeah, sweetheart?"

"Promise you'll stay this time... Promise you won't go."

"Neither of us are going anywhere, Jetty." He kissed my face gently, all the while fucking into our joined fists. "You're my little girl. I'm going to take damn good care of you."

"*Promise me*, Daddy."

"I promise," he said. "Daddy loves you, Jetty."

Lights and colors burst behind my eyelids. I moaned again and again, my muscles flexing around his fingers, my clit pulsing under his thumb. His hand tightened over mine as wet heat splashed onto my stomach, coating our hands and the undersides of my breasts.

The sound of our panting filled the air around us. Mason palmed my swollen folds and kissed my brow. I felt heavy and light, dizzy and rooted, convinced I'd float away if I wasn't holding on to him. I straightened so I could kiss his mouth, sweetly and softly, like shy teenagers skipping class to go make out under the bleachers.

He used his T-shirt to clean the semen from my breasts and belly. That's when I noticed the faint tinge of pink coating his fingers. He must've torn my hymen. Had I even noticed? In that moment, all I could recall was the pleasure.

I licked a drop of cum from my knuckle before he could mop it up; it tasted like seawater. The look on his face told me there would be plenty more where this came from, if I wanted it.

Of course I wanted it.

"Daddy," I said, my voice hoarse. "I want you to be my first in everything. Not just this."

I brought his hand to my lips and kissed his fingertips one by one. He watched, riveted. I nibbled the pads of his fingers and then sucked one into my mouth.

He inhaled sharply. "Fuck..."

I rolled my tongue along the underside and tightened my cheeks, thinking of his cock. Big and thick and solid. One thing I knew for certain. Now that I'd had a taste, I would never be satisfied until I gorged myself on him.

There was no coming back from what we'd done.

"Jetty, if we do this, we can't tell anyone. Not your mother, not your friends."

I released his finger with a wet pop. "I would *never* tell Mom about us. And as for my friends, I'll just tell them I hooked up with some guy I met this summer."

"Maybe that's what you should do." He pursed his lips, like the words tasted sour. "You deserve to meet a nice, normal guy. Someone you can kiss and hold hands with in public."

"Who says we can't hold hands?"

I twined my fingers with his. He studied our joined hands.

"Sweetheart, to the rest of the world, you're still my daughter."

"And dads and daughters hold hands all the time." I understood why he'd want to keep my mom in the dark, at least for a while; she was hardly his biggest fan. But all this secrecy seemed like an unnecessary hassle. I was an adult now. Even if she found out, there was nothing she could do about it. "Wouldn't it be easier to just tell everyone the truth?"

His expression darkened. "No, it wouldn't."

"Why not?"

He aimed his gaze somewhere far away. "If it got out that you and I were a couple, there'd be a media frenzy long after we set the record straight. I don't care if they come after me, but I won't have them putting you under a spotlight."

Something in his stare made me think he wasn't telling the whole truth.

"Daddy, I don't care about—"

"I care," he said firmly. "I love you, but I can't have you stirring up bad publicity for me."

His words hit like a slap. Yet, judging by the glint of pain in his eyes, they'd hurt him just as badly. Mason was a high-profile artist, but even this new rich and famous version of him didn't strike me as the type to give two shits about what was written on his Wikipedia page. This wasn't about avoiding bad publicity.

It was about keeping a secret.

And I could think of only one reason he wouldn't want the truth about us to come out.

"You don't want my real father to find me," I said.

He sighed heavily, the hardness in his gaze softening.

"There she is, my clever girl."

We were right back where we'd started the day before, only this time, I didn't know how to feel. Annoyed, betrayed, resentful? Sure. Baffled that someone could love me so much and still manage to lie to my face? It was hardly the first time.

"You said you didn't know who my real father was."

"I don't." He kneaded the back of my neck. "Not for sure."

"But you must have some idea." I took his face in both my hands and forced him to look at me. Goddamn, the man was almost offensively handsome up close. "Is my real father looking for me?"

Silence was his answer. It was my turn to look away.

"You're not going to tell me, are you?"

"What you don't know can't hurt you."

I begged to differ. He kissed my palms, one and then the other.

"Is he a bad man, my real father?"

Mason's arms tightened around me.

"He might be the worst."

I wanted to pound on his chest and demand he tell me everything, but I knew that would only lead to more frustration.

"I'm not a little girl anymore," I said. "It's not your job to protect me."

"You'll always be my little girl, so yes, it is my job to protect you." He kissed my forehead, his warm breath washing over my face. "Only you can decide if this secret is something you can live with, Jett. If it were up to me, you'd never leave my bed. But it's not up to me. Can you be happy pretending to be my daughter in public?"

If it meant I could still be his dirty little girl in private, I could pretend to be anything.

"I just want to be with you," I said. "I don't care about the rest."

"Then promise me one thing, Jetty. If you decide to stay, you give up the search for answers. No more questions about your real father, no more spying on me in dark hallways."

My cheeks burned from embarrassment. He smoothed his hand up and down my back to soothe me.

"You have to promise to leave the past where it belongs," he continued. "Let go of this obsession and focus on what's in front of you."

What was in front of me was the man I loved more than anything, offering me the world in exchange for giving up my struggle for the truth about myself. It didn't seem fair. I gazed down at our laps, at his cock resting dormant against his thigh. I'd only touched him once, but already I felt like I'd die if I didn't touch him again.

If I stayed, it would be with the understanding that I'd never find out why he left. There would always be a part of me that remained a mystery, but in return, I'd have a chance to get to know my daddy all over again.

Perhaps I'd regret setting aside the search for my real father someday. But for now, I had found the only daddy I needed.

"No more questions," I said. "Promise."

Mason breathed a sigh of relief. "Trust me, sweetheart. It's better to be kept in the dark about some things."

I wasn't sure if I believed him, but I was certain it didn't matter. I'd made my decision to stay—and I was going to make the most of it.

Reaching between my thighs, I dipped a finger into my pussy, then brushed a layer of my own wetness over my lips like gloss. My daddy groaned low in his throat as he kissed me, catching my bottom lip between his teeth.

With one swift movement, he laid me on my back, then kissed and licked a meandering trail from my mouth to my navel. He gripped the backs of my knees and spread my legs, just like he'd done in the studio.

I trembled as his hot breath washed over my folds.

"It took every ounce of strength I had not to eat

your pussy this afternoon," he said. "You smelled so fucking delicious."

I smiled. "How do I smell now, Daddy?"

"You smell incredible, baby girl." He rolled his tongue over my clit, and slid two fingers inside me. I struggled not to raise my hips off the couch. "And fuck if you don't taste even better."

Chapter Eleven

The next few weeks unfolded like a string of cutout paper hearts.

My first day of college was less than a month away. There were books to buy and supplies to shop for. I had stopped returning my mother's texts and calls. The life I'd left in New Hampshire was barely a niggle at the back of my mind.

Nothing existed outside of my daddy and me, and our secret.

Mason and I grew drunk on each other, and like all intoxicants, our desire made us reckless. Kisses stolen in empty galleries. A flash of skin or tongue. Riding in the backs of cabs coming home from parties, with his hand up my dress and his fingers inside me.

We even held hands on the subway.

But the bulk of our time together was spent in bed, always naked, always ravenous.

"Fuck, I'll never get tired of watching you grind on my cock," he growled, his fingernails digging furrows into the flesh of my hips. "You're gonna make me come, baby girl."

"No, don't," I said. "I want to suck you off so I can

taste both of us in my mouth at the same time." Hands braced against Mason's chest, I glided my pussy along his erection. I was so fucking wet—I was always so fucking wet when he was around. There was no help for it. Only surrender.

"Sweetheart," he said through gritted teeth, "you can't tell me not to come and then say stuff like that."

I laughed and then yelped as he reached around to slap my backside.

"Sorry, Daddy."

"Yeah right," he rasped. "I don't believe that for a second."

He raised his head to catch my nipple in his mouth. The wet warmth of his tongue sent currents of need zipping through my bloodstream. His back arched as I ground my clit against his sensitive cock-head. I was used to masturbating on my back. Riding Mason like this took a lot more effort, but the view was definitely worth it. It reminded me of humping a stuffed animal, only hotter and slipperier, with way more direct pressure on my clit.

"I'm close." I rocked my hips, letting the tension build. "Just one more minute."

"Whatever you need, baby girl." He teased my nipple with his tongue. The coalescing of pleasure from above and below made my stomach flutter.

"Oh, that. Keep doing that."

I closed my eyes. He sucked on my nipple until I was almost crying, then trailed a line of kisses across to my other breast. His cock throbbed beneath me. It must've been torture, holding back his own release while I used him to get myself off.

Clit pulsing and pussy dripping, I held his face in my hands and kissed him, recalling that first kiss and how it had changed everything. I rubbed my clit against him and thought about his cock, how close it was to my opening—

How all it would take was one miscalculated thrust to force it inside me...

My orgasm zapped through me like lightning. I whimpered into Mason's mouth. He slipped his tongue between my lips and tasted me, his hands clasping both sides of my ass, holding me even tighter to his hard body. He trembled with the effort it took to hold off on coming. I swallowed hard and took a moment to catch my breath.

"Okay," I said. "Your turn."

I slid down his body and grasped his cock, slick from my efforts and impossibly hard in my palm. I painted my lips with the drop of precum at the tip, then took the head into my mouth. He tasted salty and a little tangy, a flavor I'd come to recognize as my own. I bobbed my head, taking as much of him as I could fit without gagging.

"God, I love fucking that beautiful mouth of yours," he growled, his fingers grasping at my hair.

I responded by cupping his balls the way he liked them to be cupped. He made a sound that was like a moan and a snarl combined. I tongued his urethra, and his whole body trembled.

I was getting good at this.

"Careful," he said, "or you'll get a facial instead of a

mouthful."

I flashed him a wicked smile. It wouldn't have been the first time he'd lost control all over me.

Gripping his shaft, I wrapped my lips around him and resumed sucking him off, relishing the salt of his precum mixed with my own essence. I loved the sounds he made and the musky scent of his body. I knew exactly where he liked to be licked and how hard to suck.

As with everything else involving my daddy, I couldn't get enough. It was like I'd been born to do this. And I supposed, in a way, I had.

Mason's cock was thick. I had to be thoughtful about my positioning so I didn't end up with a sore jaw. His eyes never left my face. Sometimes he admitted to wishing he were a photographer, so he could instantly capture these moments without having to pause. More than once, I thought about suggesting we take pictures, but I was afraid mentioning photography would remind him of my mother. It would be like summoning her presence into the room, and I didn't want her here any more than I wanted to move back home.

His hand tightened in my hair. He was close. I could tell by his shallow breathing and the way his hips bucked with each swipe of my tongue. This was my favorite part, watching and hearing and feeling him lose his composure in the seconds before he was about to blow.

I sucked harder and faster, using my hand as an extension of my mouth. I listened for the helpless panting, felt the sudden swelling of his cock.

Hot, salty cum gushed over my tongue and splattered my throat. I swallowed. He loved it when I swallowed, and I loved anything that allowed me to take pieces of him inside me.

"Jesus," he muttered. "That was fucking intense."

I held him in my mouth as he softened, then let him slip out. Quiet as a cat, I crawled up the bed and settled into the crook of his arm. He pulled me close and kissed my forehead, my right cheek, then my left.

"Fuck baby," he said. I'd come to learn that excessive swearing before, during, and shortly after orgasm was just one of his quirks. "How'd you get so good at that?"

I nuzzled his neck. "I have a patient and thorough teacher."

"If only every student exhibited your boundless enthusiasm."

It was true. I had taken to practicing the art of the blow job like mastering a new artistic medium, always ready and eager to drop to my knees, and not just in the bedroom. Likewise, Mason was an expert at pleasuring me with his mouth. He could make me come in under three minutes using only the very tip of his tongue. But he much preferred to draw it out, to watch me sweat and squirm.

"What time is it?" he asked.

I grabbed his phone from the bedside table. "Almost five o'clock."

"We really should get up." He rolled on top of me and sighed, burying his face in my hair. "Remind me again why we should get up."

"Because no one can live on sex and post-coital cuddling alone?"

"I'm willing to test that theory if you are."

I laughed, relaxing into the feeling of being pinned in place by his body.

We did in fact have plans to meet up with a small group of Mason's colleagues for dinner. After an early start in the studio—he preferred morning light for painting—we'd spent the afternoon alternately napping and making love. I used to cringe at that phrase. *Making love.* It sounded so hokey. But that's exactly what we were doing, transforming desire into something tangible with our bodies. Mason's love was alchemy. He made me into something else, like new growth after a forest fire. Supple, yet strong.

The first night we spent together, he joked that he'd created a monster and we laughed about it, but it was true. I thought about sex all the time now. I wanted it every second of every day.

"I was thinking I'd invite everyone back for drinks tonight," he said.

"Sounds fun." I skimmed my fingernails down the center of his back and relished the exhale that followed. He kissed my neck, then rose from the bed, his hair wild and chest sheened with sweat—his and mine.

He smiled. "I could paint a picture every day for the rest of my life, and never paint anything half as beautiful as my little girl."

My skin tingled as though his words had physically touched me. He studied me a moment longer, then headed into the bathroom to shower. I stretched out like a starfish on the bed and listened for the sound of water beating against the tile. I'd join him in the shower in a minute. For now, I simply wanted to lay there and marvel at how this had become my life.

I'd fallen in love with the man who was once my father.

It was like a bomb had gone off inside me, forever altering the landscape. Nothing would be the same again. We'd done things to each other that I hadn't known were doable, yet we'd somehow managed to hold off on the one thing I craved more than anything.

I was still a virgin, technically speaking, but for how much longer?

Not too long, I hoped.

At first, Mason had insisted we wait until I was on birth control. When I suggested condoms, he thanked me for reminding him to go get tested for STDs. Then he said he wanted my first time to be something special. I told him every day with him was special, so could he please hurry up and fuck me before my pussy imploded.

That one earned me a time out in the studio with a box of crayons and a bowl of fruit.

I couldn't help it. I was cock-hungry. He made me feel edgy and desperate, like my consciousness had been shrunk down and relocated to my pelvis. I didn't like feeling desperate, and I didn't understand why he was holding back.

Mason's phone vibrated on the nightstand,

wrenching me from my thoughts. Feeling nosy, I checked to see who had texted him and then instantly regretted it. The text was from Krista, the model whose job I'd taken over when she'd come down with the flu a few weeks ago.

I knew he'd been sleeping with her before I came to New York. In the text, she claimed to be feeling much better, and she wanted to know if he was free for a *private party* tonight, followed by two question marks and a winky-faced kiss emoji.

I thought about deleting it. I even fantasized about how satisfying it would feel to erase every trace of her from his phone. But that would be petty and childish, and I was working so hard to prove I could be mature. I marked the message as unread to hide the fact that I'd been snooping and laid the phone on the bedside table.

I tiptoed into the bathroom and slipped inside the walk-in shower. Mason smiled when he saw me, his skin frothed with body wash.

"You got a text a few minutes ago," I said, trying to sound casual. The masochistic parts of me wanted him to check his phone as soon as he toweled off so I could ask him about it.

"Who was it from?" He moved aside to let me stand beneath the rain head. "Someone asking about dinner?"

"I didn't check."

Mason had intentionally left Krista off the guest list for every party or outing he organized, mostly for my comfort. Though he assured me he had zero interest in resuming their sexual relationship, he understood why having her around bothered me.

I washed my hair while he rinsed himself off, then stood still for him as he lathered up my body. Pressing my palms to the warm tile, I moaned softly as he smoothed the almond-scented soap over my breasts and belly, along my arms and back, then lower, rounding over my hips and thighs. He cupped my pussy with one hand and used the other to wash my backside and cleft. I gasped at the throb of pleasure that pulsed through me when his fingers met between my legs.

"You sure you don't know who it was from?" he asked, drawing soapy circles over my already sensitive clit. He'd become exceptionally good at reading me, not that I was adept at hiding my feelings. My mother had always been a champion at subterfuge; you'd think I would have picked up a few tricks after having lived with her for eighteen years.

He teased the skin around my back entrance. A warm shiver hurried down my spine.

"I don't mind if you check my phone," he said. "I know you can't resist. But I'd prefer that you tell me the truth when I ask."

Heat rushed to my face, though I couldn't tell if it was from embarrassment or arousal or both. I'd been making an effort these past few weeks, trying to prove I was as grown-up as I looked. He had to have seen it, how hard I was working to act like a responsible adult.

His finger prodded my back entrance, and my

muscles tightened instinctively. No one had ever been inside me like that before. Not even me.

"It's okay, baby girl. I promise I won't be upset." He continued to stroke me, undeterred by my body's involuntary urge to shut him out. "Just tell me the truth."

The truth smoldered on my tongue like an ember. I bit my lips together.

Once again, he tested my opening. I wanted so badly to let him in, to trust that he'd meant it when he said it was okay that I'd snooped. It was the sort of crime my mother would've held against me for months. But Mason wasn't my mother. He was my daddy, and he loved me unconditionally, the way a parent is supposed to.

My breath whooshed out of me, and his finger slid inside.

I moaned, catching water in my mouth.

My skin prickled as though I'd been electrified. I was alive and open, sensitive all over. I felt each drop of water and every inch of his finger.

Mason's cock stirred against my hip. He continued to rub my clit with his free hand, which made me want to rock my hips. Forward to chase the pleasure, backward to revel in the forbidden feeling of having my asshole breached.

"It was from Krista," I confessed. There was no point in trying to hide from him now that he was inside me. "She invited you to a private party tonight... Do you wish you could go with her?"

"Of course not." He kissed my temple. "I'm

exactly where I want to be. Besides, we already have plans."

I wanted that to be the end of our conversation about Krysta, but I was still burning with questions. "What did she mean by 'private party?'"

Mason's touch wavered as though his mind had wandered and come back around. He sighed heavily. "Krista and I have occasionally invited others to join us. But that's all in the past now."

"Oh." The thought of being passed between two lovers made me want to press myself harder against him—that was, until I understood the implication of what that meant for him and Krista. Not only had they fucked, but they'd fucked *creatively*, while Mason had yet to put his cock in my pussy even once.

"You look mildly scandalized." He withdrew from my rear and then returned with two fingers.

I opened my mouth to the spray to wash down the taste of bitterness. Pressing my full weight into my palms, I spread my hands flat against the tile and turned to look at him.

"I'm not scandalized," I said. "Just...confused."

"How so?"

"You've had threesomes with Krista, but we still haven't...you know."

He kissed my cheek, then whispered into my ear, "You like the idea of being shared?"

My pulse jumped. "Maybe..."

"You want to know what it's like to feel twice as many hands on you? Twice as many cocks begging for your attention? One here—" He moved faster in and out of my asshole. "—and another here?"

He slid two fingers into my pussy. I moaned. He was obviously trying to distract me from the fact that we hadn't fucked yet; I was embarrassed to admit it was working.

Illicit images played out like a slideshow across my mind. Four hands gliding over my hips and breasts, two mouths kissing and licking my nipples. Two cocks sliding in and out, using me, filling me to bursting. It was depraved and brutally comical, considering I had yet to have one man's cock inside me, yet here I was greedily lusting for two.

My inner muscles clenched around Mason's fingers, in front as well as behind. He was hard again. He hummed as I grasped his cock in my soapy hand. I needed this, needed his body and the reassurance of his desire for me. Especially after learning the juicy, albeit resentment-inducing, details about his history with Krista.

"Fuck me," I begged. "Please, fuck me, Daddy. My ass or my pussy, wherever you want. You don't have to come inside me. Just fuck me."

He groaned into my ear, picking up the pace with his fingers. I grappled for something to hold onto, but the tile was too slick, so I used his shoulder. He withdrew his fingers from my pussy and turned me to face him him, trapping his erection between us. We kissed, wet and sloppy.

I could practically taste his desperation.

Grasping his shaft, I guided his cock between my legs. He rocked forward, gliding against me.

This was it. He was finally going to fuck me.

He slid his fingers out of my backside and angled his cock back against my belly. The sigh that seeped from his chest had to have left him hollow.

"Not yet," he said.

He may as well have been standing on my chest.

"Why not?" I asked, my voice barely a squeak above the rushing water.

He cradled my face.

"We don't have time, sweetheart."

Liar, I thought. We'd had the past three weeks, plus the rest of our lives, and at least an hour till dinner. We had all the time in the world.

I wilted as he kissed my forehead and detached the shower massager from its post on the wall. My skin humped with goosebumps as he rinsed the soap from me, then from himself.

I didn't find the will to speak again until he'd finished toweling me off.

"Are you going to respond to her text?" I asked.

"No." He wrapped the towel around my shoulders and then motioned for me to sit on the edge of the tub so he could comb my hair. I sighed, soothed by the gentle pick and swoosh through the strands.

I left him in the bathroom to finish getting ready. My first week in New York, Mason had asked his housekeeper to move his winter clothes into storage to make room for my things. I'd convinced him to continue his work on the painting regardless of whether he intended to ever show it. After a few sessions, he presented me with a credit card with my name on it and said, "Modeling for me is work. You deserve to be compensated."

I used the money to buy myself clothes I could wear to parties and gallery openings. Gauzy shirts and backless dresses, garments that would make it easy for him to touch me whenever he wanted. Tonight, I opted for a slinky deep-violet dress with an asymmetrical hem, black lace-trimmed panties and no bra.

Standing at the full-length mirror, I knew I'd made the right choice when Mason's hands came around to softly pinch my nipples through the fabric.

Our eyes met in the glass, his gaze hot enough to warm my cheeks.

"If I haven't ripped this dress off you by dessert, it'll be a miracle."

Chapter Twelve

Mason kissed me one last time as our black car pulled up to the restaurant. Once inside the dimly lit bistro, I recognized his agent Michelle and her husband Kurt seated at a large leather-lined booth beside an artist couple I met my first week in New York.

"You're looking very charming this evening," Kurt said to me as I slid into the booth, his gaze centered on my nipples.

Tension rolled off of Mason like distant thunder as he pulled me close. I lived for these intimate moments: his arm curved around my waist at gallery openings; his hand pressed to the small of my back at his artist friends' summer homes. Caresses that in isolation would seem perfectly innocuous to anyone watching—so much so that the men we encountered didn't think twice about hitting on me.

"When people see us together they don't see a couple," Mason had lamented on our way back from a party last weekend. "They see me and they see my daughter. I've caught their mouths watering and watched their cocks perk up at the sight of you. And short of playing the overprotective-father card, there's not a goddamn thing I can do about it."

His gaze narrowed at Kurt across the table.

"How astute of you to notice," he growled.

"What a gorgeous dress!" Michelle added, diffusing some of the tension. It was hard to tell if she was genuinely oblivious to her husband's wandering eye, or simply resigned to look the other way in an effort to keep the peace.

I smiled at her. "Thank you."

"Mason," she said, "as soon as your girl has a finished piece, I want you to call me. Any time, day or night."

"In other words—" Kurt winked at me. "—she wants first dibs on your freshman thesis, just in case your father's talent is hereditary."

"Don't make fun." She slapped her husband's arm. "I've been in this business long enough to know that talent is just as much nature as it is nurture. It would be a tragedy to see even an ounce of that talent wasted on school."

Mason squeezed my shoulder. I leaned into his side. There was, of course, no way I could've inherited his talent, but I had been soaking up his wisdom on technique and composition since I arrived. He motioned for the waiter and placed a generous order of wine for the table and an array of tapas-style dishes.

Two other couples joined us, plus a few stragglers on their way back from a concert. Mason's popularity was more than justified, but it was easy to spot the difference between folks who genuinely adored his work versus those who simply wanted to boast about having dinner with Mason Black.

An hour into the meal, we were about to order another round of drinks when a familiar blonde strutted up to the table dressed in a baby-pink top and leather pants.

"So sorry we're late," Krista said. A lanky musician type with long, greasy hair sauntered in behind her looking bored. "I forgot Dez had a show in Brooklyn."

The artist couple rose from the table to kiss Krista's cheeks. Her gaze flittered toward Mason, and the lack of surprise on her face told me everything I needed to know: she knew he would be here tonight.

"It's so good to see you." She leaned across the table, aiming her kiss for his mouth instead of his cheek. He dodged her affection deftly. Still, it took everything I had not to shank her with the cheese knife. "It feels like it's been forever since we got together."

He smiled politely. "It has been a while."

Michelle motioned for the couple next to her to make room for the new arrivals. Krista and her companion scooted along the bench until they were directly across from my daddy and me.

She caught my hand before I could tuck it away.

"Jett, it is so nice to finally meet you. Your father's told me so much about you."

"Likewise." I bared my teeth. As far as I knew, he hadn't spoken to her since she came down with the flu. Had he invited her here tonight without telling me? "Are you feeling better?"

"Yes, thank goodness. I'm so bummed I wasn't able to work with your father on his current project. It sounded really special."

"Wait." Michelle turned to Mason. "I thought you were using Krista for this project."

Mason downed the remaining glug of wine in his glass and then poured three fresh glasses for himself and the newcomers. "Sadly, Krista was unable to—"

"He's painting me," I said.

Krista nearly choked on her Merlot. I smoothed my lips together to stop myself from meeting her look of horror with a grin.

Mason's hand tightened on my thigh. He was not happy with my outburst, that much was obvious, not that I could blame him. I was out of control. Something reptilian slithered beneath my skin, provoking an itch I couldn't scratch without tearing myself and everything around me to pieces.

"Wow, that's..." Krista blinked repeatedly. "I've done my fair share of nude modeling over the years, but I'm honestly not sure I could ever do something like that. I mean, pose for my own father...like that."

"Pose how?" Michelle asked. Clearly, Mason hadn't filled her in on the details of his newest painting.

"I've only seen the preliminary sketches," Krista said, "but from what I remember they were very graphic."

"My father's been sketching me since I was little," I said matter-of-factly.

"Well yeah," she said, "but surely not like this."

The entire booth seemed to hold its breath. Mason nudged my foot under the table.

Tread carefully, baby girl.

I smiled. "Obviously not."

Krista laughed softly, trying and failing to conceal her lingering discomfort. "Knowing your father's work, the shock factor of you being his daughter is just part of the appeal. Right, Mason?"

He kept his expression neutral. "I never do anything for shock value. And certain aspects of the project have changed since we last spoke."

"Not too many aspects, I hope." Michelle was practically licking her chops at the prospect of a scandal. "Nothing makes the critics salivate like good, old-fashioned controversy."

***

Safely enclosed within the low-droning quiet of the hired car, away from eager eyes and ears, Mason cupped my chin in his hand and asked, "What were you thinking, Jett?"

All I could do was shrug as he searched my eyes for answers I wasn't ready to give.

"I told you how it had to be when this whole thing started. As far as everyone else is concerned, you're my biological daughter." His voice was surprisingly cool considering how frustrated he was. "You told me you could live with that."

"I guess I'm a liar, just like you."

I turned from him to stare out the window.

"Look at me, Jett."

The disapproval in his gaze was almost sharp enough to pierce my bubble of resentment. Then I pictured Krista on her knees with a look of ecstasy on her face as Mason's cock sank into her undoubtedly bleached asshole. I crossed my arms defensively, wishing I could collapse in on myself like a dying star, brilliant and destructive.

"Sometimes I forget you're still a teenager," he said. "Then you cop an attitude, and I'm reminded just how young you are."

This, coming from the man who had been missing-in-action for most of my adolescence, whose last memory of me before he left was of a gangly pre-teen in braces shouting, *See you next weekend, Daddy,* from the driveway. He had no idea how much or how little I'd matured, and no clue how his disappearance had stunted me emotionally.

Time stopped the day I realized he was never coming back. It didn't start again until the day he kissed me.

"You don't seem to mind how young I am when I'm sucking your cock," I snapped.

"Watch your mouth, little girl," he growled, his eyes flitting to the partition separating us from the driver.

"Or what? You'll give me something to suck on?"

"Don't act like you wouldn't enjoy it."

I would've enjoyed it, but I wasn't about to agree with him.

"Where the hell is this attitude coming from?" he asked. "Don't tell me this is about Krista. She and I are ancient history."

"Then how did she know where to find you to-night?" As much as I didn't want him to know I was jealous of his former model, I needed to hear the truth from his own mouth.

"She probably asked Michelle or one of the others. We still run in the same circles."

"But you've been talking to her," I snapped. "She said you told her about me."

"I did tell her about you. The day you arrived, when she came to look at my preliminary sketches, and long before that. Lots of people know about you, Jetty."

My hard outer shell began to crumble at the sound of his nickname for me. I fought with myself to stop it from shattering completely. "You had no idea she was going to be there?"

"If I had, I would've cancelled on the group and taken you to dinner somewhere else." He cradled the back of my head in his big, warm hand. "Krista is no more important to me than an old piece of furniture. There's nothing to be jealous of—"

"Of course there is! You fucked her."

There it was... the real reason for my biting anger. This wasn't about Krista; I knew in my bones that Mason would never cheat on me. It was about us, me and him, and the one thing he refused to give me.

He sat back against the leather seat, his expression hardening. "I see what this is really about. You want something, and you're throwing a tantrum because I won't give it to you."

In what felt like a single fluid movement, he unbuckled both our safety belts, slid to the center of the backseat, and bent me over his lap so that my face was pressed to the leather. He pulled my dress up and my panties down, exposing my ass to the air.

The first slap was a shock to the senses, like an upward gunshot or the crash of a gavel. It hurt. It burned. It stopped my thoughts in their tracks.

"You've been a bad girl, Jetty." He held me tightly as I squirmed, the bulge of his erection demanding my attention through his slacks. He was enjoying this, and to my utter amazement, so was I. "A *very* bad girl."

The little hairs on the back of my neck stood on end. He hit me again on the opposite side, then again where he'd spanked me first. My pussy fluttered with every slap. He spanked me twelve times in all, six firm smacks on each rounded cheek.

Tears flowed freely down my face, not from the pain, but from release.

I couldn't believe how easily his touch had disarmed me, or the speed with which he had reduced me to a sorry little girl. In a way, the spanking had simplified things. I was no longer a spiteful teenager seething with jealousy. I was a brat in desperate need of punishment.

Somehow, he had known that what I really needed was a taste of Daddy's discipline.

"Now," he said, "what do you have to say for yourself?"

He caressed my tender flesh. I sniffled.

"I'm sorry."

"Sorry for what?"

"Sorry for being a brat—and telling everyone about the painting." I let out a sob. Mason shushed me gently, his fingers gliding between my legs from behind to caress my mound. His touch was both sexual and not, the way a hug or a kiss or a slap could go either way depending on who was giving it.

"It's all right, sweetheart. I forgive you." He righted my clothes as we pulled up to his building, then raised me up to kiss me. That was all it took to rekindle my desire for him. I laid one hand on his cock and wrapped the other around his neck as he slid his tongue into my mouth.

The car slowed and then stopped. I didn't want to leave the warmth and privacy of the backseat, but the driver was waiting.

"Come on," Mason rasped, taking my hand. "I need to get you naked."

We hurried through the lobby toward the private penthouse elevator, ignoring the front-desk attendant who tried to snag our attention. Nothing was going to stand between us and where we wanted to be: pressed against each other, skin to skin.

Before the elevator doors slid shut, Mason had me pinned against the mirrored wall with his hand between my thighs. He tugged my panties to the side and slipped two fingers inside me.

"You are the most important thing in my life," he said between kisses. "I need you to trust that I know what's best for you."

"I trust you, Daddy."

He fucked into me with his fingers, using his thumb to stroke my clit. My pulse raced as he whispered in detail all the ways he was going to make me come tonight—

All the ways except the one I was dying to hear.

The elevator doors slid open onto our floor. Distraught and out of my mind with desire, I reached for the only leverage I had left.

"If you don't fuck me now," I said, "I'll take this elevator back down and you'll never see me again."

His hands left my body in an instant. He took a giant step back, then another, all the way into the hall.

"Well," he said, "what are you waiting for?"

Regret squatted in the back of my throat. I tried to swallow it down, but the lump refused to budge.

"Shall I book your flight?" he asked. "Hell, I'll even help you pack your bags if that's what you want—"

"You know that's not what I want."

"I know you're not going to get anything by trying to manipulate me."

The gravity in his stare made me feel three feet tall. I moved toward him, out of the elevator, just as his phone began to buzz in his pocket.

"I'm sorry." I reached for him but he didn't reach back. My eyes burned with tears. "I don't know why I said that."

"You said you trusted me to know what's best."

"I do trust you, completely. But it's not fair. You won't fuck me, and you won't tell me why you won't fuck me."

"I'm trying to protect you."

"I didn't ask for your protection," I said a little too forcefully. "What could you possibly protect me from by coming in my mouth instead of my pussy?"

His phone buzzed again. This time, he snapped it up to answer it.

"What?" He paused, listening.

Anxiety coiled in my belly as I watched the emotion drain from his face.

"Send her up," he said.

He tucked his phone back in his pocket and disappeared into the apartment. I followed. He didn't bother to take his shoes off as he strode to the kitchen to pour himself a shot of brandy.

"Who's coming?" I asked when it became clear he wasn't going to volunteer the info. I swore, if Krista stepped out of the elevator, I was going to lose it.

He downed the drink he'd just poured, refreshed the glass, then slid the shot over to me.

"Looks like we're about to have a family reunion."

Chapter Thirteen

I wished I could step back into the memory of the last time I saw my father before he left me. I would've used the opportunity to look for signs, clues, smoke signals. Anything that might've hinted at his impending disappearance.

Whenever I tried to comb through the memories, the details blended together until I wasn't sure if I was remembering the right film we saw, or the flavor of ice cream in my cone.

To my twelve-year-old self, everything about that day had seemed normal.

What I did remember was the look of relief on my mother's face when I walked through the door, as if she'd half expected to never see me again.

I wondered if Mason ever considered running off with me. I used to imagine how differently my life would've unfolded if he had. Would we have circled the globe ten times over, only to find ourselves at a similar crossroads between my estranged parents?

Maybe this was all inevitable. Absconded from my mother, or abandoned by my father, the outcome would've been the same: a life shrouded in secrets.

The fruitless search for the disparate parts of myself. All roads converging on this exact moment in my father's foyer.

My mother stepping out of the elevator, looking tired and harried, yet beautiful as ever.

"Hello, Jett." She clutched a brown-paper shopping bag in front of her like a talisman against some perceived evil.

"Mom," I said. "What are you doing here?"

"You won't return my calls, so I thought I'd come to you." She scanned the foyer, her gaze lingering on the open door to the studio. "I'd like to speak with my daughter *alone*."

"You can talk in the apartment," Mason said. "I'll be in my studio—"

"Is there some reason we can't talk in there?"

She didn't wait for him to respond before she stepped inside. Mason shot me a look of apprehension before he followed. I trailed behind them both, noting his gaze flickering toward his work in progress. Thankfully, only the back of the canvas was visible from this side of the room.

"The apartment would be more comfortable," he said.

"This will do fine. I'm not staying long."

My mother stood ramrod-straight, forcing Mason to walk around her on his way to the door. My own spine felt about as sturdy as dried spaghetti in comparison. He lingered in the doorway; his expression guarded.

"You're sure you don't want me to stay?" he asked

me.

I shook my head. I could handle my mother alone; after all, I had six years of training under my belt. Mason sighed; his gaze wary.

"I'll be in the apartment if you need me," he said, then shut the door.

My mother and I assessed one another in the resulting silence. She was wearing the silk scarf I'd given her last Mother's Day over a striped dress that emphasized her waifish figure.

"Have you been crying, Jett?"

I sucked in a loud breath through my nose. "It's nothing."

"It doesn't look like nothing." She looked me over with a small, sad smile. "Is that a new dress?"

I nodded.

"It's nice," she said. "You look good."

My mother's eyes appeared sunken, like she hadn't slept in days. I wondered if she'd stopped eating, and if I asked her, would she tell the truth. She set her purse and the shopping bag on the floor and opened her arms to me.

"Can I get a hug?"

I remained rooted in place. I didn't want her to touch me. I was convinced she'd be able to read the truth on my skin like Braille. She gave up on the hug after a few seconds, her smile tightening into a wince as she tucked a lock of hair behind her ear—hair the same color and thickness as mine, only shorter.

Guilt rapped its knuckles on the back door of my heart. I pinched the inside of my wrist, both as penance for treating her coldly and to distract myself.

"Do you want to show me what you've been working on?" she asked.

It seemed like a safe enough way to fill the silence. I shrugged. "Okay."

Thankfully, I didn't have to go far to gather my sketchbooks. My mother stepped up to the workbench, and I laid my drawings out for her perusal. She fingered the pages with care, her gaze drifting over depictions of clouds and random body parts, distant cityscapes.

"These are lovely." She lingered over a series of sketches featuring my daddy's hands holding and manipulating various objects: paintbrushes, bedsheets, flowers, my feet. "These are Mason's hands."

"Um...yeah," I said. Apparently, time plus wear and tear in the studio hadn't altered his hands so as to make them unrecognizable. I was glad I'd known better than to store the drawings of his cock with my regular sketches.

My mother cleared her throat but said nothing in response. You could fill volumes of empty pages with everything she'd left unsaid over the years. Grimacing, she pressed a hand to her stomach.

I had to ask. "When was the last time you ate?"

She breathed through what appeared to be an intense abdominal cramp. "I had coffee this morning."

So, this was how she was going to punish me for not staying in touch. By refusing to take care of herself. I clenched my jaw. "I'll get you something from the apartment—"

"No," she snapped. Then, more calmly, she added, "I have a granola bar in my bag."

Hands shaking with frustration, I snatched her purse from the floor and rifled through it until I came across a fruit-and-nut bar. She took her time opening the package, and even more time forcing herself to take a bite.

Her gaze flitted about the studio as she chewed. I counted my breaths. *One. Don't see the painting. Two. Don't ask what Mason's been working on—*

"Is that Mason's newest piece?" She pointed to the back of the large canvas by the window. The one that, on its front, depicted her teenage daughter masturbating with no clothes on.

"It's not finished," I said, trying to sound detached. "He doesn't want anyone to see it yet."

She took a few steps toward the painting. My heart kicked against my sternum. I shadowed her, grabbing her hand before she could reach the easel.

"He doesn't like people to see his work before it's done."

She tugged free from my grasp and continued on, determined. Short of physically restraining her, there was no way to stop my mother from seeing the painting.

I hugged myself as a bolt of panic ripped through me like lightning. Bile washed the back of my throat. If she saw it, if she assumed the truth and confronted me about what we'd done... I was going to lose it.

If my body were a house, my mother would be the tornado blowing the roof off its frame and tearing the doors from their hinges. She rounded the easel and then abruptly stopped.

She cupped a hand over her mouth.

"Oh, God... No."

The look of abject horror on her face made my stomach coil in on itself.

"It's not what you think," I said, though I had a feeling it was indeed exactly what she thought. "His model called in sick. I offered to take her place."

"And he let you?" Her voice was pure agony. The sound of it made my stomach cramp, like a child wailing after hearing its mother's screams. Tears streamed down her face. "I knew this would happen. I knew it."

"Knew what would happen?"

My mother wiped her cheeks and turned to the window like she couldn't stand to look at either version of me.

"Just tell me the truth. Has he touched you?"

"You mean like, a hug?" Even now, I was still desperately clinging to the hope that I could spin this, that I could somehow convince her the painting was the extent of our physical relationship.

"Don't play dumb, Jett. Has Mason put his cock inside you?"

I nearly burst into giggles at the realization that Mason's restraint—infuriating as it was—had inadvertently saved me the burden of lying.

"No, he hasn't."

I wasn't sure if she believed me but asking would only undermine my insistence.

She made her way back to the workbench, giving

the futon a wide berth, as if its presence alone was enough to make her sick. She cried silently for over a minute, then rubbed her eyes and said, "This is all my fault. I should've told you what he was, why I made him leave."

"Why did you make him leave?" I moved around to the opposite side of the workbench so I could look straight at her.

"He didn't tell you?" She choked out a laugh.

"Well someone had better tell me, because I'm sick of being kept in the fucking dark about my own childhood."

I stood across from her and waited. I waited a long time. Finally, she wiped the tears from her cheeks and met my gaze.

"I made Mason leave, to protect you."

A shiver scurried up my spine as six years' worth of pain and anger lodged in my throat.

"Protect me from what?" My voice trembled. "He might not be my real father, but he was a good father to me. What were you so afraid of?"

She reached beneath the table and pulled out the shopping bag.

"See for yourself."

Chapter Fourteen

My mouth went dry as cotton. This was it, one piece of a puzzle I had come all this way to put together.

Was I ready to see the whole picture?

Hesitantly, I reached into the bag and pulled out a stack of sketchbooks. The pages were old and frayed around the edges. I took a deep breath and drew back the cover on the top book. The pencil lines were smudged from having been compressed, but the shape they made was unmistakably that of a sleeping child.

"Who is this?" I asked.

"It's you."

I turned the page. There I was around the age of two in duck-themed pajama bottoms, then again, clutching a stuffed clown fish. Me wrapped in moon-and-star sheets with one foot off the mattress, my head just south of the pillow.

I closed the first sketchbook and moved on to the next. It was the same thing. Sketch after sketch of me asleep, first in my old twin bed, then in what appeared to be my father's bed, from the time I was little to around the age of eleven.

"Mason drew these?"

My mother nodded.

I watched myself grow up across the pages, saw my limbs lengthen and my hair darken, my face and figure sharpen. Back then, my father couldn't afford the most spacious living arrangements, so he would crash on the couch and let me sleep in his bed. He would've had to have been slipping into his room to draw me every weekend, quiet as a ghost, for over a decade to capture this progression.

"I knew you were sitting for him during the day," my mother said, wringing her hands like she was trying to squeeze the blood from them. "I thought that was the extent of it. Then I found a sketchbook in the trunk of his car—he'd let me borrow it while mine was in the shop. I saw that he'd been drawing you in your sleep. The thought of him sitting there, watching you in the dark while you were helpless made me...uncomfortable, to say the least."

The bottom sketchbook was only halfway full. I recognized the pajamas I was wearing in the first drawing from the year I'd turned twelve—the same year Mason had left without so much as a *Catch you later*.

"I asked Mason how long he'd been drawing you at night," she said. "He told me not long, a few months. I said I didn't want it to happen again, and he assured me it wouldn't. A few weeks later, I stopped over at his place to pick something up and I found these. He'd lied to me."

I flipped to the very last drawing: me on my stom-

PRETTY, DARK AND DIRTY

ach with my arm dangling off the edge of the bed and my hair fanned out across the pillow. Obviously, my father had been coming in to draw me a lot longer than just a few months. But surely that wasn't enough of a reason to banish him forever.

"That's it? He lied to you about drawing me?"

"It was enough."

I squinted at the pages in front of me. "I don't understand."

My mother closed her eyes and pressed three fingers to her lips. She looked fragile, more so than usual, like she'd shatter if I tried to pick her up.

"I didn't grow up like most people, Jett. My parents were wealthy—and I don't just mean they were rich. I mean we had old money. Our house was a historic Victorian mansion sitting on hundreds of acres of untouched land that'd been handed down for generations. We had a name that meant something to the town we lived in."

She pressed a hand to her stomach, then took another bite of granola bar, chewed and swallowed.

"My mother homeschooled me for ten years," she continued. "After she got sick, my father hired tutors, music teachers. I didn't meet anyone who wasn't a relative or an employee the entire time I lived there, and I only left the property once when my appendix burst."

I stood with my mouth hanging open. I'd never heard the story of my mother's upbringing, and hearing it now, I could hardly wrap my brain around the strangeness of it.

"My father let most of the staff go after my mother died. The place became a tomb. The housekeeper could hardly keep up, so she closed off the parts of the house that no one used. I used to sneak into the old drawing room to get away from—"

She closed her eyes.

"To get away from what?" I asked after a long stretch of silence.

"Our groundskeeper demanded my father let him hire an assistant to help with the mowing. That's when Mason came to live with us, in the grounds-keeper's cottage. He was nineteen. I was fifteen. He was the only person remotely close to my age I'd ever met besides my cousins, and we hardly ever saw them."

My mother began to pace, scuffing her boots with each sharp turn. She looked deep in thought, like she'd fallen down a rabbit hole inside herself. The next time she spoke, it was like a levee had burst, and the only way out was through her mouth.

"We were broken people, Mason and me. His mother had given him up for adoption, and the foster-care system hadn't done him much better. Of course, my father forbade him to speak to me. That lasted all of a week. We began seeing each other in secret. Then I got pregnant."

My whole body went taut. Pregnant?

"Mom, are you saying..."

"I couldn't raise a child in that house," she continued, ignoring me. "I knew we had to leave. I told Mason my father would kill us both if he found out we'd been sleeping together, so we made a plan to run away. We left the day after my sixteenth birthday."

My stomach plummeted twelve stories.

"It was harder than I thought it would be," she said. "I couldn't stand crowds and I couldn't hold down a job. But Mason took care of us—all of us. He swore he would never let his child starve, and he kept that promise."

"Mom, are you saying... Is Mason my real father?"

She turned to look at me. "Would it be so terrible if he was?"

I had to brace my hands on the table to stop my knees from buckling.

"But you said he wasn't." I clamped my mouth shut. I couldn't let her see how much the possibility that Mason was in fact my father had rattled me—and was *still* rattling me.

"Honestly, I wish I hadn't said anything. Maybe if I'd gone on letting you believe he was your real father, you wouldn't have let him get close enough to abuse you now."

"He's not abusing me." I was so fucking confused. "Mom, for once in your life, please just tell the truth. Is Mason my real father, or isn't he?"

She gazed down at her hands, which had begun to shake. I rounded the table to take her hands in mine.

"Please Mom," I begged. "I need to know."

My mother's throat shifted as she swallowed. "I was seven years old the first time my father raped me. When I told my mother what had happened, she said I was just having a bad dream. I tried to tell her again and she slapped me. She knew what he'd done, and she did nothing to stop it."

"Oh... Mom." My stomach revolted at the thought of my mother being violated by the man who was supposed to protect her—

Her father. My grandfather. My mother's rapist.

Bile washed the back of my throat. I dropped the sketchbook and ran to the sink just in time to vomit into the steel basin.

My thoughts ran in circles. *It can't be true. How can it be true?* But I knew in my heart that it was. Acid burned my throat. My mother gathered my hair into a makeshift plait, stroking my back the way she used to when I got sick to my stomach after eating too much candy. When the nausea subsided, I rinsed my mouth and the sink, then turned to face her.

"I'm sorry," I whispered.

She took my hands in hers. This was the most forthcoming she had ever been with me, and I could tell it was taking everything she had not to crumple in on herself like a dying spider.

"It didn't happen all at once," she said. "It started when I was little, the slow chipping away at my boundaries. We were so isolated... I thought it was normal. By the time I met Mason, my father was raping me almost every night. I wanted to tell him, but I was scared he wouldn't believe me." Her voice cracked. "You believe me, right, Jett?"

"Of course I do." I pulled her into a tight hug. She felt like a sprite in my arms, like she could sprout fairy wings and fly away.

"Don't you see?" She left my grasp, coming to stand before the pile of sketchbooks. "When I found these, I realized what I'd thought was a healthy fascination was actually the makings of a sick obsession. I was so scared for you. I told Mason to leave immediately and cut off all contact with you, or I would take these sketches to the police."

Glancing back at the very last drawing, I tried to see it as anything other than a charcoal study of a sleeping figure. But I could find nothing sinister in the portrait, nor in any of the others, nothing to differentiate them from the kind of drawings I'd be making in art school. It had to be the sheer volume of them—pages upon pages of sprawled limbs tangled in rumpled bedsheets—that had struck a nerve with my mother.

To the untrained eye, these drawings could look criminal. But I knew better. What my mother had gone through wasn't the same as me and Mason. For one thing, he'd never forced himself on me. For another, I wasn't a child. I was old enough to make my own decisions.

"Mason told me I was insane to think he'd ever hurt you," she said. "But even if he hadn't touched you, that didn't guarantee he wouldn't someday. Turns out I was right."

My thoughts swirled like water circling a drain. As far as I could recall, Mason had never abused me. But my mother wanted me to believe that the possibility had always been there, lurking in the shadows at my bedside. That had to be what she'd hoped to convince me of by showing me these drawings.

I picked up the sketchbook I'd dropped on my way to the sink and joined her at the workbench.

"You're wrong, Mom. I am so, so sorry for what happened to you. But Mason isn't like that. He never abused me."

"Then how do you explain that?" She pointed at the painting. "What person, in their right mind, would let their child pose for them like that? What child would feel comfortable masturbating for their parent?"

"It's art, Mom. It doesn't have to make sense to make a statement. And I'm not his child."

"But you were." She took a deep breath to steady herself. "If I hadn't kept him away from you all these years, would you have let him paint you like that?"

I honestly didn't know. It was possible that I would've felt comfortable enough letting my father see me naked. It was also possible that in forcing Mason out, my mother had made us mysteries to one another, and mysteries needed solving.

"It doesn't matter," I said. "I'm here now, and I feel good about it."

My mother's eyes brimmed with tears. "Every decision I have made was for your protection. I took you far away from the only home I'd ever known. I gave you another man's name. I became a single parent overnight, and I never asked for one cent of Mason's money. Now, I'm not asking for gratitude, but could you at least respect my sacrifice?"

"You forced my father out of my life based on a

hunch and threatened to use his own art against him. I'm fucking devastated for you, Mom. I really am. But it sounds to me like Mason made the bigger sacrifice."

My mother flinched as though my words had physically hurt her. A small part of me was glad. I blamed her for separating me from my father, and then I felt awful for blaming her, and then I didn't know what to feel, so I felt nothing and then everything.

She wiped the tears from her eyes. "Can't you see that he's just using you to punish me? That painting is a slap in the face. My face."

I scoffed. How typical that she would try to make his painting of me about them, as if our relationship was merely an offshoot of something they'd started. "That doesn't make any sense. You weren't even supposed to see it."

"Jett, wake up! Of course I'm supposed to see it. Everyone is going to see it. Shining a light on things that should be private is what Mason does."

I needed to step back, to reclaim some space, to remind myself that I wasn't as trapped as I felt and that I still had a choice. To believe her or not. To remain here, in this room, or not.

"You won't understand," my mother said. "Not until you have children of your own. Not until you have to look into the face of the man you love and ask yourself if he's really a monster."

I stared her down. "Mason is nothing like your father. He loves me. We love each other. He would never hurt me. You're wrong about him now, just like you were wrong about him back then."

"For your sake, Jett, I hope I'm wrong." Her bottom lip trembled. She leaned forward, as if gazing deeper into my eyes might help her see the truth more clearly. "If it's not too late, if he hasn't already fucked you, do yourself a favor and get out while you still can. Because once you cross that line, it changes you. There's no going back."

I'd never seen my mother cry more than a few solitary tears before tonight. Now it was as though the floodgates had opened, allowing a rare, unguarded glimpse at a person I'd spent my whole life struggling to know. I saw the defenseless child and the hardened, distrustful teen, the overprotective mother burnt by the past and terrified of the future.

She stood before me vulnerable and exposed, as she must have the day she'd told her own mother what her father had done—the moment her mother had chosen to side with a monster against her own child.

"I had hoped to bring you home tonight," she said. "But I see now that you have no intention of letting me help you out of this situation."

I pushed past the twinge of revulsion and frustration corkscrewing through my belly. "Because I don't need help, Mom. I'm okay."

She shouldered her purse, took one last plaintive look at me and said, "Take care of yourself, Jett, since you obviously have no interest in letting me take care of you anymore."

Chapter Fifteen

I watched my mother leave and then sat on the futon with my head in my hands and my heart in my throat. Another wave of nausea washed over me, followed by a flood of pity. Pity for my mother and everything she had gone through, and for the havoc her decisions had wrought upon the lives of those closest to her.

My father hadn't wanted to leave me. It was my mother who'd pushed him out. Because she wanted to keep me safe from the shadow of the man who had hurt her.

Of all the potential reasons behind Mason's abandonment, I had never considered anything like this. I felt wrung out like a rag, limp and useless. I wanted to wrap myself around him and let the strength of his body support me. I wanted to press my ear to his chest and listen to his heartbeat. The slow, dependable throb I'd come to rely on to lull me to sleep.

I rinsed my mouth again and took a moment to dry my eyes before returning to the apartment. Mason stood at the kitchen sink, staring into the drain as though hypnotized. I approached him slowly.

"Mom told me who my real father is," I said. He

closed his eyes. "She says she was raped by her father... My grandfather."

Mason let out a long breath as he reached for me. I let him pull me close.

"I'm so sorry, Jetty." He cradled my head in his big, warm hand. "I can't imagine how difficult this must be for you."

"Did you know?"

His body tensed in the seconds before his reply. "Not for sure. But there weren't a lot of men in your mother's life at the time, which left only a few possibilities."

My eyes burned with tears. I'd thought I was done crying; apparently, I was mistaken. I clung to him like a small child as he lifted me up and sat me down on the kitchen counter.

"None of this changes who you are, Jetty." He kissed my trembling lips. "You're your own person, and you're a *good* person. What that evil man did has no bearing on who you are now."

I desperately wanted to believe that.

"It's going to be all right," he said. "I'm going to reach out to a few people, find you a professional who can help you get through this."

The thought of talking to anyone about the awful truth made my skin crawl. "Can't I just talk to you?"

"You can always talk to me. But your first semester of college is going to be hard enough without the shadow of this ugliness hanging over you."

"I just want to forget I ever knew any of it." I sobbed into his chest. He smoothed my hair and rocked me gently in his arms.

"I wish you didn't have to know any of it, sweetheart. And I wish I knew the right things to say to make it all better. But you need to process this, otherwise it'll haunt you. I'll make some calls in the morning."

He held me as my sobs tempered into sighs. I doubted I'd ever feel comfortable talking about the things my mother had told me, but Mason was right. If I tried to bury the truth, I'd end up just like her: cold and bitter, a body haunted by secrets and shrouded in lies.

"Well," I said, trying to sound chipper, "at least now we can tell people you're not really my dad."

"We will, I promise. But not just yet. If the bastard is still alive, he might try to find you. I want to know where he is before we say anything." He dried my tears with his thumbs and then kissed both my cheeks. "I'll kill the fucker with my bare hands before I let him come within a ten-mile radius of my little girl."

I couldn't help smiling at the possessive tone his voice had taken. I was still his little girl, even though we both knew where I'd come from. He kissed me gently on the lips. I tried to deepen the kiss, but he pulled back, his expression restrained.

"What else did Gretchen tell you?"

I didn't want to talk about the drawings or why she'd made him leave, because as far as I was concerned, there wasn't a drop of truth to it. But I didn't want to lie to him, and a lie of omission is still a lie.

"She told me why you left," I said. "She even

brought your old drawings for me to look at. I think she thought seeing them would make me feel differently about you, which is ridiculous."

Mason closed his eyes and took a step back. Something in the air around us shifted, as though a sinkhole had opened up between our feet.

"People hear the word love and automatically think sex," he said. "You were my daughter and I loved you. You were beautiful, so I watched you. Photography wasn't my forte, so I found other ways of capturing you. I would've sooner put a bullet in my head than let anyone lay a finger on you, including me."

He rounded the kitchen island. With every step, I felt him slipping away, like air leaking slowly from a balloon.

"Maybe it was for the best that I had to stop drawing you," he said. "Being scrutinized like that when you're still growing into yourself has to be tough. At least you got to have a normal adolescence."

If normal meant happy and well-adjusted, then there'd been nothing normal about my adolescence. "You really think I was better off not knowing why you left or where you'd gone?"

"Compared to the alternative? Yes. Leaving you isn't something I'm proud of, but it beats having to tell your twelve-year-old that her mom thinks you're a pedophile."

The abject pain in his voice hit me like a sledge-hammer.

"I thought about fighting it," he said. "But if you weren't my biological kid, I had no legal standing.

Then I imagined what a big court battle would've been like for you. Having to answer a bunch of disgusting questions about our relationship, not to mention the possibility that other people would see what your mom saw in those sketches. I didn't want to put you through that, and I sure as hell didn't want you to have to carry it around."

I hopped down from the counter and went to him, taking his face in my hands. He pressed his cheek to my palm but kept his arms at his sides. I kissed his face and tried to kiss his lips. He slipped away before our mouths could meet.

"Maybe you should've gone home with your mother," he said.

My stomach seized. "You can't mean that."

"Jett, I've spent the last six years telling myself I was in the right, that your mother was just paranoid. Then you show up here and... I can't even say it."

He let me take his hand. "Weeks ago, when I asked you if my father was a bad man, you said he might be the worst. Were you talking about yourself?"

"Does it matter?"

"Of course it matters! Mom's wrong about you. You're *nothing* like him."

"I don't know what I am anymore. When I saw you at the museum it was like waking up after having been asleep my whole life. Then later, in your room, when you asked for a hug and I was finally able to hold you, I couldn't get close enough."

A twinge of loss skittered up my spine as he pulled his hand away. I wanted to snatch it back, to staple it to mine so he couldn't pry us apart again without drawing blood.

"I got hard that night just thinking about your mouth," he said.

The divot between his brows looked deeper than I was used to seeing. I was giving him wrinkles. *Good*, I thought. *Let me mark his outsides as permanently as he's marked my insides.*

"You know the saying, when something is so wrong it feels right?" he asked. "This wasn't like that at all. It didn't feel wrong, which I guess tells us all we need to know. You might not be my biological daughter, but I was your father for twelve years. And I'm exactly what your mother thinks I am."

My mother had called him a monster.

And if anyone had firsthand experience with monsters, it was her.

I wanted to crawl out of my skin thinking about what her own father had done to her as a child. Still, that didn't mean she was right about Mason.

"You're both wrong," I said. "She thought you were going to abuse me, and that's not what this is at all. We love each other. We just love each other *differently* than most people."

"Differently is one way of putting it."

I pressed both hands to his chest. "Is that why you won't have sex with me? Because you think it'll prove her right?"

"What I've already done has proven her right a thousand times over." He guided my arms to my sides and then kissed my forehead, as if that simple fatherly gesture were enough to soothe me.

He pulled an envelope from his jacket pocket and laid it on the countertop.

"What's this?" I asked.

"A paternity test. Technically you need a judge or a physician to order one for you in the state of New York, but I had my lawyer pull some strings."

I turned the envelope over. "It's opened."

He nodded. I ran my fingers along the jagged edges of the torn white envelope, marveling at how something so small and innocuous could terrify a big, formidable man like Mason.

"Gretchen already lied to us once," he said. "I wanted to be sure before we did something we couldn't take back."

I didn't need to ask him what the results were. I already knew the truth.

He plucked the envelope from my hands.

"Then," he continued, "I realized I was missing the point. It doesn't matter that I'm not your real father. I was a father to you for over half your life. I never should have let you come here, let alone touched you. I'm sorry I let you believe I could be the man you needed."

Panic wrapped itself around my heart at the finality in his words. "But you are. You're exactly what I need!"

"No, sweetheart." His voice splintered. "You deserve someone who's capable of loving you like a normal father should."

"I don't *want* a normal father. I want *my* father. I

want you."

A small spark of hope ignited and then fizzled in his eyes.

My mother had been dead-wrong about him, but she was right about one thing: there was no going back for either of us. It didn't matter if he never touched me again. We'd altered each other irrevocably, like paint swirled on a palette. You couldn't take violet and separate it back into blue and red. Once the colors were blended, all you had was purple.

I reached for him, and he guided my hands away. Once again, my eyes flooded with tears. I fought to keep them there, convinced that I wouldn't be able to remain standing if he saw me crack again.

But I was already broken.

As desperate as I was to be with him, I couldn't bear the thought of Mason hating himself for loving me too much, or too intensely, or whatever my mother would accuse him of next. We were either in this together, completely and shamelessly, or not at all.

I tore the envelope from his grasp and ripped it in half.

"I don't care what the test says. You think seeing it on paper makes a difference, but obviously it doesn't. You'll always find another excuse to push me away. You say you can't love me like a normal father. Then don't. Love me like a father and a lover and a mentor and everything else, because I need all of you. And if you can't give me that, then I guess I can't have any of it. Because being loved halfway hurts too much."

As impossible as it felt to turn away from him, I somehow managed to make myself go. Mason caught my arm, his grip tight enough to pinch.

"Jett, wait—" For a second, I thought he was going to kiss me. *Please*, I thought. *Kiss me. Tell me to stay*. I held my breath and waited for him to make the right choice.

He released me.

A sob shook my chest. There was no stanching the flow of tears now.

I wiped my eyes and stepped away from the man who'd been Daddy for so much of my life, the man who looked like he'd aged ten years in the last ten seconds.

"At least I got to say goodbye this time," I said. "That should count for something."

Chapter Sixteen

I cried in the shower, and while brushing my teeth, and then went to my room to cry some more. Not the master bedroom where Mason and I had slept together, but the guestroom he brought me to that first afternoon.

There wasn't much point in shutting off the light, since I knew I wouldn't be sleeping, but I welcomed the darkness anyway. Part of me wished I could crawl back into the dark, where my parents had put me. Had I known the truth would be this devastating, I wouldn't have fought so hard to drag it into the light.

It was a lie I could almost believe.

When I promised Mason that I would stop asking questions, a part of me knew I could no more give up my desperate search for answers than I could command myself to stop breathing. The truth always had a way of unearthing itself, no matter how deeply you buried it. My mother knew that better than anyone.

The other lie I'd been feeding myself since the day I arrived was that I'd forgiven Mason for walking out of my life in the first place. In truth, I had only set aside my pain and anger. It wasn't until I learned the real story, and saw the anguish on his face, that I was able to truly forgive him—not exactly the reaction my mother had hoped for in coming here, that much was obvious.

But my forgiveness was irrelevant as long as Mason refused to forgive himself. In my naiveté, I'd assumed that learning the truth would bring us together. Instead, it only served to wedge us further apart.

I pressed my face into the pillow to muffle the sounds of my mewling. My father was about to exit my life again, only this time, it would be me walking out the door.

As close as we were—which was admittedly closer than we would have been if he hadn't left in the first place—it wasn't close enough to bridge the gap between the man he was and the monster he was terrified of becoming.

In the end, maybe we were both monsters for wanting what was forbidden.

I rolled onto my side and watched the lights flicker in the windows of distant apartment buildings. I almost didn't hear the doorknob creak and click.

Footsteps padded softly all the way to the bed.

My pulse jumped.

Was he here to make one last drawing of his sleeping daughter before she erased herself from his life?

A slight draft hit my back as the covers lifted. The mattress dipped. Mason's warm body spread out alongside mine, solid and consoling. I wanted to press against it, to align myself with the wall of hard muscle, but I was afraid I might not have the strength to crawl out of bed again if I did.

I had meant what I said about the pain of being loved halfway.

Maybe I could've settled for a normal father-daughter relationship before, but now that I knew how it felt to be kissed and touched and desired by him, there was no pretending that *normal* would ever be enough.

He caressed my arm, the heat from his hand soaking into my skin. "Want to know the hardest part about being a parent?"

I shrugged one shoulder.

"Most of the time, you still feel like a kid yourself. You have no fucking clue what you're doing, but you're supposed to know what's best for this tiny, fragile creature that's hellbent on getting itself into all kinds of trouble."

He tucked his leg between my calves and wrapped his arm around my middle. There was no telling where his body ended and mine began.

"Sometimes dads fuck up," he said. "I know I've fucked up more times than I can count. You'll always be my baby, Jetty. I'll never stop looking out for you. But you've got a good head on your shoulders and a bold heart filled with love."

He pressed a kiss to my shoulder. I swallowed the small stone in my throat.

"You're the only one who can decide what's right for you." Though his tone was unquestionably sober,

I couldn't ignore the persistent ridge of his cock pressed against my backside.

"What if the things that are right for me feel wrong to you?" I asked.

He hummed low in his throat as I ground against him. For sure, his body wanted the same things mine did. It was his mind that needed convincing.

"Maybe it's time we redefined the terms." He slid his hand under my tank top to stroke my abdomen, sending warm chills skittering throughout my nervous system. "I swear, I never wanted anything like this when you were little."

The insistence in his voice broke my heart all over again. It was a statement he shouldn't have needed to make, though I understood why he felt he had to say it.

"I believe you," I said.

His lips brushed my neck. "The day you were born was the second-happiest day of my life."

"What was the first?"

He smiled against my skin. "The day you came back to me."

Everything I thought I'd lost came rushing back—the familiar sense of safety and comfort, sharpened to a fine edge by an insatiable hunger. I craned my neck to grant him access to my mouth. He kissed me as though he were in danger of drowning and my breath was the only thing keeping him afloat. His hands slid up into my shirt to cup my bare breasts.

"You're the greatest thing I ever made." He may not have made me with his own body, but he'd undoubtedly had a hand in molding me into the woman I'd become. "I can't lose you again, baby girl. I *won't* lose you."

I turned in his arms so I could look at him. "I don't want to lose you either. But I won't be the reason you hate yourself."

Lights from outside washed his face in cool blue tones. He stroked my side, his expression looking more resolute by the minute. Still, I didn't want to get my hopes up.

"I could never hate myself for loving you the way you deserve." He kissed the tip of my nose, his warm breath washing over my cheeks in gentle gusts. "And you deserve to be with someone who can love you hard enough for two."

Some girls were lucky enough to have both a father and a lover, two distinct streams of affection. Somehow, I had managed to tap into both streams from the same man. It wouldn't matter if I had a thousand lovers after him, none could ever love me as deeply or intensely as he did.

"So love me harder, Daddy."

I felt his cock twitch against my thigh through his boxers; I loved that I could do that to him, make his body crave my touch without even trying. Mason had captured me from every angle, awake and asleep, naked and clothed. Yet somehow, he still couldn't get enough of me.

His mouth claimed mine in a kiss that stole the air from my lungs and the words from my lips. My nipples stiffened as he lifted my shirt to expose my breasts. Easing me onto my back, he dipped his head to take my nipple into his mouth. My clit pulsed like a heart beating between my legs, as he teased my breasts with his tongue. I ran my hands over his hair, pulling gently, then harder when his teasing devolved into torture.

"Please, Daddy. I need…"

I was at a loss for words. He gazed up at me, his darkened stare grasping mine and refusing to let go.

"What do you need, baby girl?"

"I don't know. Something. Anything." I licked my lips. "I just need you."

Mason helped me pull my shirt off, taking a moment to admire my nakedness before he scooped me up to straddle his lap. I latched onto him like a thing possessed, pushing my breasts against him. He gripped my hips and rocked his erection against me, sending sharp pulses of agonizing desire straight to my bones.

We kissed like our survival depended on how thoroughly we could wear out our tongues.

I couldn't take the ache inside me any longer.

Reaching between us, I freed his cock from the confines of his underwear. After a few exploratory pumps, I yanked the crotch of my underwear aside and guided him to my folds.

"Patience, baby." He chuckled softly—a most infuriating sound if there ever was one—and caught my wrist in his hand.

I nearly sobbed with frustration.

"But you said—"

"I only meant, if we're going to do this, we're going to do it right."

He laid me down on the bed and kissed my jaw, then my throat, continuing in a straight line down my chest and stomach, pausing only to lick a circle around my belly button.

Gooseflesh pricked across my skin in the wake of his mouth. As exasperating as it felt to be put off yet again, I had a feeling he was about to make it worth my while. He slid my panties off, wrapped his arms around my thighs and settled between my legs.

I'd lost track of the number of times we'd done this, but the hunger in his gaze when he saw my pussy for the first time always made me shiver. He parted my lips and planted a kiss just above my clit. My blood turned to honey in my veins, slow and sweet and golden. I wanted to kiss him, but he was too far away, so I nibbled on my fingers instead.

He traced my inner labia with the tip of his tongue and then fucked into me. I gasped as his nose met my clit. His tongue delved deeper. I writhed, my hips lifting off the bed as my inner muscles tightened.

"Too much?" The tilt of Mason's smile made it clear he knew exactly how much—or how little—it took to make his little girl flail around like a fish on the dock.

I went limp as he dipped his head to lick my pussy from top to bottom.

He flattened his tongue and lapped languidly, focusing on my clit. I closed my eyes and surrendered to the feeling of having my bones turn to gelatin.

His tongue flicked and fluttered before easing into a steady rhythm. A warm, welcome flush swept through me. My nipples pebbled, aching to join in on the fun. I massaged my breasts, ratcheting my pleasure even higher. His tongue disappeared for a second and then returned, along with two slick fingers. He teased my opening, then slid inside.

I cried out at the delicious intrusion, melting like ice cream in the summer sun.

He sucked my clit softly. Tiny eruptions of pleasure lit up my brain like fireworks. He added a third finger, fucking into me while his lips and tongue worked their incredible magic.

"Oh God... That feels..." I couldn't hold the words in my head long enough to say them out loud. My arousal crested. I felt the urge to bear down, to clench up, to be everywhere at once.

I came around Mason's fingers, my arms and legs tensing. He fixed his mouth over me, playing with my clit and stretching out my orgasm until it all became too much and I had to wave him off.

He flashed a glossy smile. "I fucking love making you come, sweetheart."

"Me, too." I grinned languidly. "Thank you, Daddy."

"My pleasure, baby girl."

He wiped his face with the sheet and then crawled up to kiss me. He'd left a thin sheen of arousal on his lips just for me. I savored the delicate tang.

His cock nudged my belly, spreading a drop of pre-cum above my navel. I took him in my hand, stroking lightly and coaxing a low growl from his throat.

"Christ, my balls feel like dead weight." He groaned as I swirled my thumb around the tip of his cock. "I want you so fucking much. Too much. I don't want to hurt you."

I cupped his jaw and forced him to meet my gaze. "The only way you could hurt me now is by making me wait another second."

His mouth curved into a knowing smile. He laid his palm between my breasts, over my heart, then skimmed his fingers down to cup my mound. Arousal bloomed fresh between my thighs. I whined softly. His gaze darkened as he palmed my swollen flesh.

Please, I thought, *don't give yourself a chance to over-think it.*

I pressed against him, needy and insistent. He reached for his cock. My heartrate picked up speed as he positioned the head at my folds.

"Put your arms around me," he said. "And tell me if anything hurts."

Thousands of tiny moths took flight inside my ribcage. I clutched at his back and shoulders as he slid the head of his cock inside me. My muscles burned. He withdrew to the very tip and then eased forward. I inhaled sharply.

"Am I hurting you?"

He was, a little, but I didn't mind. "Not really."

His shoulders tensed. "Want me to stop?"

"No, keep going." I squeezed my eyes shut.

"You sure?"

I nodded. I wanted this, all of it, the pain as well as

the pleasure.

Mason kissed a meandering trail from my ear to my lips. He eased his cock a bit further inside me and then paused, allowing me time to get used to the new sense of fullness. I imagined supple, receptive things: roses blooming, sand slipping through spread fingers, dark-chocolate pudding. I willed myself to remain open, to embrace the anticipation of not knowing what would happen next.

When his pelvis met mine, I knew he was all the way inside me. I felt stretched, plugged, so full I thought I'd burst. Still, it didn't hurt nearly as much as my friends had said it would. Then again, weeks of fingering and oral sex had no doubt prepared me for the main event.

I felt every inch of his cock sliding in and out, every inch of my pussy expanding and contracting around him. But it wasn't enough. I needed more pressure on the outside, more direct stimulation of my clit.

I opened my eyes. Mason was watching me, his expression equal parts lust and concern.

"What do you need, baby girl?"

I wetted my kiss-chapped lips.

"My clit," I said.

He sat up without pulling out. Draping my legs over his thighs, he gripped the backs of my knees and hauled me toward him, burying his cock deeper inside me. I moaned, shaken by the sensation and turned on by the unparalleled view of his toned chest and stomach. He licked the pad of his thumb and then used it to stroke my clit while he fucked me.

I came undone.

"Oh my God," I stammered. "Oh shit. Oh fuck..."

This was it. Exactly what I needed.

My muscles gripped him tighter. So tight I was sure I'd force him out. But he kept on thrusting, his own string of expletives tangling with mine as he bucked his hips. Fucking me harder. Faster. It hurt a little at first, but then it began to feel wonderful.

I wasn't used to having something that big inside me while I got off. It was kind of disorienting. He switched from circling my clit to strumming. I cried out as he pounded into me, drifting somewhere between agony and ecstasy and loving every second.

"You feel amazing sweetheart," he said. "Are you close? Tell me how to make you come baby. I want us to come together."

The awareness that my father was about to come inside me was enough to coax a second orgasm from my already spent body. Rather than respond, I simply let the sensation take me: deep, throbbing bass notes —deeper than I was used to—coupled with the sense of total fullness.

I opened my mouth, but no sound followed as my pussy clenched him like a fist. Tight and tighter.

My orgasm seemed to go on forever.

"Jesus fuck, baby." He drove into me, his abdominal muscles flexing with every thrust.

His cock pulsed. He was coming inside me. Not on my breast or my stomach or in my mouth, but in my pussy. Where no other man had ever come before.

This was it. This was everything.

I came again.

A low roar clawed its way up Mason's throat as he thrust into me one last time. Wetness trickled down from where our bodies met, dampening the sheets beneath my ass. We gazed at one another through love-drunk eyes, both of us sweat-sheened and out of breath. My limbs felt sluggish as I reached out to touch his hands, still clamped to my outer thighs.

The gravity of what we'd just given each other pulled at us until we couldn't hold ourselves up any longer. He dropped his weight into his elbows, as I wrapped my arms around him and kissed his neck.

His heart pounded against my chest like firm knocks on a door, but I couldn't have opened myself further if I tried. Besides, he was already inside me. In more ways than one. My heels dug trenches into the backs of his thighs as I clung to him, wanting to keep him there, to make him a permanent part of myself. He cradled my face as his cock softened and then shifted onto his side.

"How are you feeling?" he asked.

There were too many emotions and not enough words to describe them, so I settled for, "Different."

"Good different or not-so-good different?"

"Very good different." I hardly recognized my own voice, ragged and breathy and sounding impossibly young.

His breath washed over my chest, making my nipples tighten. "I'm glad. I was worried you might feel..."

"Feel what?" I traced his collarbone with my

fingertip and fought to keep my eyes open. I needed to stamp this moment into my memory like a block printing, so I would never forget the slip-slide of my inner thighs, or the berry-red shade of his lips.

He closed his eyes. I tugged on his earlobe.

"Feel what, Daddy?"

"I was afraid you might regret it."

The apprehension in his gaze nearly broke my heart. After everything, he was still afraid I was going to change my mind about him.

I shifted closer to his body, nestling into the angle between his chest and the bed.

"Never," I said. "It was everything I could've hoped for, and so much more."

"You have no idea how happy that makes me, Jetty." He kissed me with a passion that belied the sleep in his voice. "I love you so goddamned much. I'd be fucking devastated if you left after all that."

"I love you, too. And you don't have to worry because I'm not going anywhere without you."

His cock stirred against my thigh. Straddling his hips, I rocked my pussy back and forth against his growing erection, coaxing it back to its full hardness. But instead of the usual pussy job I used to give him, I angled his shaft upward and then sank down.

We both gasped, Mason's fingernails biting into my flesh like blunt teeth.

"Jesus," he said with a smile, "my little girl's insatiable."

I bent to nibble his ear and whispered, "Just like her Daddy."

Epilogue

❧

Three months later.

"This is bullshit!"

My painting teacher, Professor Mendez, massaged her temples with her fingertips. "Please calm yourself, Stefan, or I'm going to have to insist that you leave us."

Stefan pointed an accusatory finger in the face of the guy seated next to him.

"My painting isn't derivative," he shouted. "Your ugly face is derivative. And the rest of you are all a bunch of mindless hack drones who wouldn't know real art if it took a dump on your chests."

He grabbed his painting from the easel and hurled it to the linoleum. A few people gasped, others laughed. I rolled my eyes.

"Take a walk Stefan," Professor Mendez said. "A *long* walk."

"Whatever." He stormed out of the classroom, pausing only to wipe his shoes on his *real art* and almost falling down in the process.

"There's one every semester." Professor Mendez shook her head and then gestured to the next painting, a grayscale portrait of a sleeping couple entwined on a bed. "Now, what do we think of Jett's piece?"

The seconds piled like sand at the bottom of an hourglass. I'd lost track of the number of times I had started, stopped, and scrapped the painting. I met my new friend Sasha in Ceramics Club my first week at NYU. She and her boyfriend Alister had been good sports about posing for the painting, willing to strip down and cuddle up whenever I needed a visual reference, their enthusiasm waxing and waning in direct correlation to my offers of free burritos.

"It's intimate," said a girl with magenta hair, "yet, there's resistance. You can see the desperation on their faces, like they're trying to hold onto each other."

"The way she plays with light and shadow is really effective," said a wiry guy whose name I could never remember. "It makes the bedding and the people's skin look three-dimensional."

"Does anyone recall the term for that?" Professor Mendez scanned the group. No takers. "Chiaroscuro. Modeling in light and dark to make objects appear solid."

"I think she could've done more with the background," said the first girl. "The walls are totally bare. It feels unfinished."

"But I think that's the point," said another girl with thick-rimmed glasses. "It keeps our focus on the couple."

Professor Mendez moved on to the next piece, and I let my shoulders relax. I studied my painting a moment longer, noting the tweaks I would've made and the things I would've taken better care with if only I'd had more time.

It's done; time to let it go, Mason would say, and he'd be right. The critique was over. In fact, my professor had probably already assigned it a grade.

We finished up with minimal tears shed, after which Professor Mendez wished us all a good weekend and cut us loose.

"Jett," she called just as I was leaving. "May I speak with you for a moment?"

I hoped this wouldn't take long. I had an appointment with my therapist scheduled for after class, followed closely by Mason's art show—his first in over three years.

I joined Professor Mendez in front of my painting and tried not to make it obvious that I was itching to go.

"I told you at the start of the semester that I wasn't going to go easy on you just because your father is Mason Black," she said. "But I'm pleased to say, you've impressed me all on your own."

I smiled. "Thank you, Professor."

"I heard your father has an opening in the East Village tonight. The gallery owner is a friend of mine. Maybe I'll see you there."

A little trill of anxiety skittered up my spine. I had no idea what to expect from Mason's show tonight. He'd insisted on keeping this series a surprise. For all I knew, he was planning to debut the watercolor close-ups of my pussy he'd painted last fall.

That would be awkward.

I hustled the few blocks to my therapist's office, arriving only a couple of minutes late. Dr. Kelley had my usual cup of green tea waiting for me on the coffee table, beside a fresh box of tissues that I would surely plow through.

It had taken more than a few sessions for me to concede that talking about my shame and anger and disgust was better than trying to bottle it up. At the same time, it took twice as many sessions for Dr. Kelley to accept that my relationship with Mason was both healthy and consensual, if a little—okay, a lot—unconventional.

We ended the appointment early so I could hustle back to my dorm room to get ready for the art show. Although I spent most of my nights with Mason, he insisted I have a private space to crash on campus. It had come in handy more than once, and we even managed to christen the tiny twin bed one afternoon between classes. Fucking on our sides with my back to his front and his hand over my mouth to catch my moans. It didn't matter how many times my daddy fucked me; his love had a way of making me feel brand new.

Half an hour later, with my hair straightened and lips stained candy-apple red, I squeezed into a white lace dress and a pair of red pumps before heading out.

The gallery, a hip, modern space with walls that didn't quite reach the vaulted ceilings, was already teeming with people when I arrived. I recognized most of the pieces from Mason's collection, still life paintings of antique children's toys and sketches of my body—throat, earlobe, the arch of my foot. Lines clean and crisp, yet impossible to distinguish unless you knew my body as well as he did.

I said hello to Mason's artist friends, then went to stand with his agent, Michelle.

"You must be really pleased with how this all turned out," she said.

I nodded. "I was with him when he bought some of those old toys."

Her brow crimped. "You haven't seen the main exhibit?"

"There's another exhibit?"

Michelle smiled and captured my arm. "Come with me."

She steered me through the crowd toward a wide archway leading to an interior space I hadn't realized was there.

"This has to be some of his finest and most personal work yet," she said.

I steeled myself for the reveal.

We waited for the mob to dissipate, then stepped inside the enclosure. The walls were covered in drawings of children.

No, not children. One child. Me.

They were the drawings from my father's sketchbooks—the ones my mother had returned—blown up, sharpened, splashed with color and arranged with care.

My heart swelled like a balloon.

"They're remarkable," said Michelle, squeezing my hand. "He's titled the series *Lost and Found.* You can really feel how much he loves you in every piece."

I nodded, unable to speak.

Suspended from the ceiling were three full-length sketches that had been blown up and elaborated to make them appear three-dimensional. At the center of the room lay another 3D rendering of a very small, sleeping me curled around a stuffed rabbit that was almost as big as I was.

My eyes stung with tears. Mason had given me that rabbit. I was pretty sure my mom still had it somewhere, packed alongside other beloved keepsakes from my childhood. It broke my heart that I couldn't just call her up to ask for it.

I dabbed my eyes with the napkin Michelle handed me. "Where's he now?"

"Upstairs being interviewed by a journalist from the New York Times. He should be finishing up soon. I'll let him know you're here."

"Thank you."

She squeezed my hand again and then left me to take in the exhibit on my own.

I circled the room slowly, floored by how Mason had succeeded in transforming something my mother had deemed criminal into the most beautiful display of tenderness I'd ever seen.

The crowd around me burst into claps and cheers. I glanced up to find Mason making his way over to me, his gaze never leaving mine, even as people tried to snag his attention. My preferred look for him would always be scruffy and paint-splattered, but damn, the man could rock a suit.

"Sorry, I was upstairs," he said. "I really wanted to be here when you saw the exhibit." He pulled me into a hug that prompted someone close to us to whisper, *Aww, that must be his daughter*.

"That's all right." I hugged him tighter. "It's incredible."

He pressed a kiss to my ear and whispered, "Not as incredible as you in the flesh."

I could almost feel his arousal thickening the air around us. My whole body tingled in response. He kept his arm around me as we circled the room, coming to stand at the center, next to a three-dimensional rendering of me as a very young child.

I leaned my head on his shoulder. "I can't believe Mom thought these were anything less than beautiful."

He kissed my temple. "You know, I invited your mother to tonight's show."

"You did?" I balked.

"She told me to go fuck myself." He smirked. "I'd say that's progress, considering she wasn't even speaking to me a month ago."

I hadn't seen or spoken to my mother since the night she came to tell me what a monster Mason was. Dr. Kelley was trying her best to help me work through my resentment toward my mother, but I was a work in progress. I didn't understand why Mason would want to have her in our lives.

"You know she'd hate all of this almost as much as

you hate each other," I said.

"I don't hate your mother, Jett."

"Why not? I would if I were you."

He squeezed my shoulder. "She gave me the greatest gift a father could ask for. That's why I can't hate her, no matter how angry I get when I think about all the years of your life I missed."

I gazed down at the younger version of me on the floor. Round and sleepy and oblivious to all the pain and confusion that would inevitably follow.

Then again, none of this, what Mason and I had now, would be possible if my mother hadn't done what she felt was necessary. If he could forgive my mother for driving him away from me, maybe I could find it in myself to forgive her, too.

She would never understand our relationship. Most people wouldn't. Our love wasn't clear and crisp like a photograph. It was messy and abstract.

It belonged on a canvas.

"I have some news." His expression turned grave. "My PI got back to me about Gretchen's father. He said the bastard ate a bullet shortly after your mom and I took off. Left his fortune to charity."

The weight of Mason's words settled over us like dirt being tossed onto a fresh grave. I waited to feel anything besides relief. As far as I was concerned, my mother's father wasn't my father. I may have come from him, but I wasn't him.

He was a monster and he'd been defeated.

"I always wondered why he never came looking for us," Mason said.

I pressed my palm to his chest. "Does this mean we can stop pretending I'm just your little girl?"

He covered my hand with his own. "You'll always be my little girl. But I won't be satisfied until I make you something more."

Without letting go of my hand, he dropped down on one knee in the middle of the gallery. The crowd around us broke out in gasps and murmurs. Someone asked if this was part of the exhibit.

"Jett, you are the love of my life. I've watched you grow from a sweet child into a strong, talented, and beautiful young woman. It would be an honor to spend the rest of my life watching you grow into yourself. Will you marry me?"

My mind could hardly process the meaning of his words. Was he serious?

Shaking myself from my stupor, I met his unwavering gaze. No, this wasn't a stunt; he meant every last word of it.

"Yes, Daddy," I said, my voice clear and confident as crystal. "I'll marry you."

I watched, mesmerized, as he tore a thin strip of paper off one of the exhibits and wrapped it around my finger.

"We'll get you a real ring tomorrow." He winked at me and then stood to take my face between his hands.

Then, he kissed me—a real kiss that made the crowd around us lose their fucking minds.

Mason scooped me up in his arms and carried me out of the main exhibit, nimbly dodging the press through the throngs of confused and scandalized attendees.

"Where are we going?" I asked.

"Upstairs, to the manager's office. I need to get inside you, and as much as I enjoy performance art, I'm not sure if this crowd could handle me taking you from behind in the middle of the gallery surrounded by pictures of you in diapers."

Laughter bubbled up from inside me as we ascended the stairs. I felt sweet and light as cotton candy in Mason's arms. He took me into the manager's office, kicking the door shut behind us, and laid me on the big wooden desk.

As fast as he could get my panties off, he was inside me.

I held tight to him as he pounded into me like he'd been blessed by the god of sex. I was more than wet enough to take him. In that moment, I knew I would always be wet enough, always hungry enough, always craving him.

And my daddy would always be ravenous for me.

"You're my baby girl, Jetty," he growled. "No matter how big you get."

"I'm yours, Daddy." I moaned as the first wave of my orgasm hit. "I'm yours."

Playlist

The following playlist served as creative inspiration throughout the writing and revision of *Pretty, Dark and Dirty*.

"Never Be the Same" by Camila Cabello
"Make a Shadow" by Meg Myers
"I'm on Fire" by AWOLNATION
"This Love" by Taylor Swift
"Hands to Myself" by Kings of Leon (cover)
"Fire Meet Gasoline" by Sia
"Hold Back the River" by James Bay
"Do You Feel It?" by Chaos Chaos
"Blue" by Troye Sivan (feat. Alex Hope)
"I Believe in Us" by Léon
"Compass" by Zella Day

FORBIDDEN NEVER

FELT SO GOOD.

Margot Scott likes long nails and short, sexy reads, rainbow sprinkles on vanilla ice cream, and rainy days spent in bed with her furbabies. When she's not writing forbidden-love stories about bearded older men, you can find her browsing Pinterest for pictures of pink things.

Visit **margotscott.com** to sign up for her newsletter.

Follow Margot on Facebook at
facebook.com/margotscottauthor

Join Margot's Facebook group at
facebook.com/groups/margotshouse

Made in the USA
Middletown, DE
18 December 2020